Solomon

by

Constance Fenimore Woolson

Double9 BOOKS

Solomon

by Constance Fenimore Woolson

ISBN: 978-93-71815-55-0

Published by

DOUBLE 9 BOOKS

2/13-B, Ansari Road
Daryaganj, New Delhi – 110002
info@double9books.com
www.double9books.com
Tel. 011-40042856

ABOUT THE AUTHOR

Constance Fenimore Woolson was an American novelist, poet, and short story writer, born on March 5, 1840, in Claremont, New Hampshire. She was a grandniece of James Fenimore Cooper, a renowned American writer. Woolson is best known for her works set in the Great Lakes region, the American South, and among American expatriates in Europe. Her writing often explored the complexities of human emotions, social settings, and the intricacies of life in both familiar and foreign landscapes. Her style combined detailed character studies with vivid descriptions of settings. Woolson's works garnered attention for their realism and insight into the lives of women. Her most famous stories reflect her interest in the social dynamics of these regions, as well as the lives of people navigating change, identity, and relationships. Woolson passed away on January 24, 1894, at the age of 53 in Venice, Italy. She was the daughter of Hannah Cooper Pomeroy, whose influence on her writing is often noted. Woolson's legacy continues through her literary contributions, especially in American fiction.

CONTENTS

SOLOMON

MIDWAY in the eastern part of Ohio lies the coal country; round-topped hills there begin to show themselves in the level plain, trending back from Lake Erie; afterwards rising higher and higher, they stretch away into Pennsylvania and are dignified by the name of Alleghany Mountains. But no names have they in their Ohio birthplace, and little do the people care for them, save as storehouses for fuel. The roads lie along the slow-moving streams, and the farmers ride slowly over them in their broad-wheeled wagons, now and then passing dark holes in the bank from whence come little carts into the sunshine, and men, like *silhouettes*, walking behind them, with glow-worm lamps fastened in their hat-bands. Neither farmers nor miners glance up towards the hilltops; no doubt they consider them useless mounds, and, were it not for the coal, they would envy their neighbors of the grain-country whose broad, level fields stretch unbroken through Central Ohio; as, however, the canal-boats go away full, and long lines of coal-cars go away full, and every man's coal-shed is full, and money comes back from the great iron-mills of Pittsburgh, Cincinnati, and Cleveland, the coal country, though unknown in a picturesque point of view, continues to grow rich and prosperous.

Yet picturesque it is, and no part more so than the valley where stands the village of the quaint German Community on the banks of the slow-moving Tuscarawas River. One October day we left the lake behind us and journeyed inland, following the water-courses and looking forward for the first glimpse of rising ground; blue are the waters of Erie on a summer day, red and golden are its autumn sunsets, but so level, so deadly level are its shores that, at times, there comes a longing for the sight of distant hills. Hence our journey. Night found us still in the 'Western Reserve.' Ohio has some queer names of her own for portions of her territory, the 'Fire Lands,' the 'Donation Grant,' the 'Salt Section,' the 'Refugee's Tract,' and the 'Western Reserve' are names well known, although not found on the maps. Two days more and we came into the coal country; near by were the 'Moravian Lands,' and at the end of the last day's ride we crossed a yellow bridge over a stream called the 'One-Leg Creek.'

'I have tried in vain to discover the origin of this name,' I said, as we leaned out of the carriage to watch the red leaves float down the slow tide.

'Create one, then. A one-legged soldier, a farmer's pretty daughter, an elopement in a flat-bottomed boat, and a home upon this stream which yields its stores of catfish for their support,' suggested Erminia.

'The original legend would be better than that if we could only find it, for real life is always better than fiction,' I answered.

'In real life we are all masked; but in fiction the author shows the faces as they are, Dora.'

'I do not believe we are all masked, Erminia. I can read my friends like a printed page.'

'O, the wonderful faith of youth!' said Erminia, retiring upon her seniority.

Presently the little church on the hill came into view through a vista in the trees. We passed the mill and its flowing race, the blacksmith's shop, the great grass meadow, and drew up in front of the quaint hotel where the trustees allowed the world's people, if uninquisitive and decorous, to remain in the Community for short periods of time, on the payment of three dollars per week for each person. This village was our favorite retreat, our little hiding-place in the hill-country; at that time it was almost as isolated as a solitary island, for the Community owned thousands of outlying acres and held no intercourse with the surrounding townships. Content with their own, unmindful of the rest of the world, these Germans grew steadily richer and richer, solving quietly the problem of co-operative labor, while the French and Americans worked at it in vain with newspapers, orators, and even cannon to aid them. The members of the Community were no ascetic anchorites; each tiled roof covered a home with a thrifty mother and train of grave little children, the girls in short-waisted gowns, kerchiefs, and frilled caps, and the boys in tailed coats, long-flapped vests, and trousers, as soon as they were able to toddle. We liked them all, we liked the life; we liked the mountain-high beds, the coarse snowy linen, and the remarkable counterpanes; we liked the cream stewed chicken, the Käse-lab, and fresh butter, but, best of all, the hot bretzels for breakfast. And let not the hasty city imagination turn to the hard, salty, saw-dust cake in the shape of a broken-down figure eight which is served with lager-beer in saloons and gardens. The Community bretzel was of a delicate flaky white in the inside, shading away into a golden-brown crust of crisp involutions, light as a feather, and flanked by little pats of fresh, unsalted butter, and a deep-blue cup wherein the coffee was hot, the cream yellow, and the sugar broken lumps from the old-fashioned loaf, now alas! obsolete.

We stayed among the simple people and played at shepherdesses and pastorellas; we adopted the hours of the birds, we went to church on Sunday and sang German chorals as old as Luther. We even played at work to the extent of helping gather apples, eating the best, and riding home on top of the loaded four-horse wains. But one day we heard of a new diversion, a sulphur-spring over the hills about two miles from the hotel on land belonging to the Community; and, obeying the fascination which earth's native medicines exercise over all earth's children, we immediately started in search of the nauseous spring. The road wound over the hill, past one of the apple-orchards, where the girls were gathering the red fruit, and then down a little declivity where the track branched off to the Community coal-mine; then a solitary stretch through the thick woods, a long hill with a curve, and at the foot a little dell with a patch of meadow, a brook, and a log-house with overhanging root, a forlorn house unpainted and desolate. There was not even the blue door which enlivened many of the Community dwellings. 'This looks like the huts of the Black Forest,' said Erminia. 'Who would have supposed that we should find such an antique in Ohio!'

'I am confident it was built by the M. B.'s,' I replied. 'They tramped, you know, extensively through the State, burying axes and leaving every now and then a mastodon behind them.'

'Well, if the Mound-Builders selected this site they showed good taste,' said Erminia, refusing, in her afternoon indolence, the argumentum nonsensicum with which we were accustomed to enliven our conversation. It was, indeed, a lovely spot,—the little meadow, smooth and bright as green velvet, the brook chattering over the pebbles, and the hills, gay in red and yellow foliage, rising abruptly on all sides. After some labor we swung open the great gate and entered the yard, crossed the brook on a mossy plank, and followed the path through the grass towards the lonely house. An old shepherd-dog lay at the door of a dilapidated shed, like a block-house, which had once been a stable; he did not bark, but, rising slowly, came along beside us,—a large, gaunt animal that looked at us with such melancholy eyes that Erminia stooped to pat him. Ermine had a weakness for dogs; she herself owned a wild beast of the dog kind that went by the name of the 'Emperor Trajan'; and, accompanied by this dignitary, she was accustomed to stroll up the avenues of C—, lost in maiden meditations.

We drew near the house and stepped up on the sunken piazza, but no signs of life appeared. The little loophole windows were pasted over with paper, and the plank door had no latch or handle. I knocked, but no one came. 'Apparently it is a haunted house, and that dog is the spectre,' I said, stepping back.

'Knock three times,' suggested Ermine; 'that is what they always do in ghost-stories.'

'Try it yourself. My knuckles are not cast-iron.'

Ermine picked up a stone and began tapping on the door. 'Open sesame,' she said, and it opened.

Instantly the dog slunk away to his block-house and a woman confronted us, her dull face lighting up as her eyes ran rapidly over our attire from head to foot. 'Is there a sulphur-spring here?' I asked. 'We would like to try the water.'

'Yes, it's here fast enough in the back hall. Come in, ladies; I'm right proud to see you. From the city, I suppose?'

'From C—,' I answered; 'we are spending a few days in the Community.'

Our hostess led the way through the little hall, and throwing open a back door pulled up a trap in the floor, and there we saw the spring,—a shallow well set in stones, with a jar of butter cooling in its white water. She brought a cup, and we drank. 'Delicious,' said Ermine. 'The true, spoiled-egg flavor! Four cups is the minimum allowance, Dora.'

'I reckon it is good for the insides,' said the woman, standing with arms akimbo and staring at us. She was a singular creature, with large black eyes, Roman nose, and a mass of black hair tightly knotted on the top of her head, but pinched and gaunt; her yellow forehead was wrinkled with a fixed frown, and her thin lips drawn down in permanent discontent. Her dress was a shapeless linsey-woolsey gown, and home-made list slippers covered her long, lank feet 'Be that the fashion?' she asked, pointing to my short, closely fitting walking-dress.

'Yes,' I answered; 'do you like it.'

'Well, it does for you, sis, because you're so little and peaked-like, but it wouldn't do for me. The other lady, now, don't wear nothing like that; is she even with the style, too?'

'There is such a thing as being above the style, madam,' replied Ermine, bending to dip up glass number two.

'Our figgers is a good deal alike,' pursued the woman; 'I reckon that fashion ud suit me best.'

Willowy Erminia glanced at the stick-like hostess. 'You do me honor,' she said, suavely. 'I shall consider myself fortunate, madam, if you will allow me to send you patterns from C—. What are we if not well dressed?'

'You have a fine dog,' I began hastily, fearing lest the great, black eyes should penetrate the sarcasm; 'what is his name?'

'A stupid beast! He's none of mine; belongs to my man.'

'Your husband?'

'Yes, my man. He works in the coal-mine over the hill.'

'You have no children?'

'Not a brat. Glad of it, too.'

'You must be lonely,' I said, glancing around the desolate house. To my surprise suddenly the woman burst into a flood of tears, and sinking down on the floor she rocked from side to side, sobbing, and covering her face with her bony hands.

'What can be the matter with her?' I said in alarm; and, in my agitation, I dipped up some sulphur-water and held it to her lips.

'Take away the nasty smelling stuff,—I hate it!' she cried, pushing the cup angrily from her.

Ermine looked on in silence for a moment or two, then she took off her neck-tie, a bright-colored Roman scarf, and threw it across the trap into the woman's lap. 'Do me the favor to accept that trifle, madame,' she said, in her soft voice.

The woman's sobs ceased as she saw the ribbon; she fingered it with one hand in silent admiration, wiped her wet face with the skirt of her gown, and then suddenly disappeared into an adjoining room, closing the door behind her.

'Do you think she is crazy?' I whispered.

'O no; merely pensive.'

'Nonsense, Ermine! But why did you give her that ribbon?'

'To develop her æsthetic taste,' replied my cousin, finishing her last glass, and beginning to draw on her delicate gloves.

Immediately I began gulping down my neglected dose; but so vile was the odor that some time was required for the operation, and in the midst of my struggles our hostess re-appeared. She had thrown on an old dress of plaid delaine, a faded red ribbon was tied over her head, and around her sinewed throat reposed the Roman scarf pinned with a glass brooch.

'Really, madam, you honor us,' said Ermine, gravely.

'Thankee, marm. It's so long since I've had on anything but that old bag, and so long since I've seen anything but them Dutch girls over to the

Community, with their wooden shapes and wooden shoes, that it sorter come over me all 't onct what a miserable life I've had. You see, I ain't what I looked like; now I've dressed up a bit I feel more like telling you that I come of good Ohio stock, without a drop of Dutch blood. My father, he kep' store in Sandy, and I had everything I wanted until I must needs get crazy over Painting Sol at the Community. Father, he wouldn't hear to it, and so I ran away; Sol, he turned out good for nothing to work, and so here I am, yer see, in spite of all his pictures making me out the Queen of Sheby.'

'Is your husband an artist?' I asked.

'No, miss. He's a coal-miner, he is. But he used to like to paint me all sorts of ways. Wait, I'll show yer.' Going up the rough stairs that led into the attic, the woman came back after a moment with a number of sheets of drawing-paper which she hung up along the walls with pins for our inspection. They were all portraits of the same face, with brick-red cheeks, enormous black eyes, and a profusion of shining black hair hanging down over plump white shoulders; the costumes were various, but the faces were the same. I gazed in silence, seeing no likeness to anything earthly. Erminia took out her glasses and scanned the pictures slowly.

'Yourself, madam, I perceive' she said, much to my surprise.

'Yes, 'm, that's me,' replied our hostess, complacently. 'I never was like those yellow-haired girls over to the Community. Sol allers said my face was real rental.'

'Rental?' I repeated, inquiringly.

'Oriental, of course,' said Ermine. 'Mr.—Mr. Solomon is quite right. May I ask the names of these characters, madam?'

'Queen of Sheby, Judy, Ruth, Esthy, Po-co-hon-tus, Goddess-aliberty, Sunset, and eight Octobers, them with the grapes. Sunset's the one with the red paint behind it like clouds.'

'Truly a remarkable collection,' said Ermine. 'Does Mr. Solomon devote much time to his art?'

'No, not now. He couldn't make a cent out of it, so he's took to digging coal. He painted all them when we was first married, and he went a journey all the way to Cincinnati to sell 'em. First he was going to buy journey all the way to Cincinnati to sell 'em. First he was going to buy me a silk dress and some ear-rings, and, after that, a farm. But pretty soon home he come on a canal-boat, without a shilling, and a bringing all the pictures back with him! Well, then he tried most everything, but he never could keep to any one trade, for he'd just as lief quit work in the middle of the forenoon and go to painting; no boss 'll stand that, you know. We kep' a going down, and I had to sell the few things my father give me when he found I was married whether or no,—my chany, my feather-beds, and my nice clothes, piece by piece. I held on to the big looking' glass for four years, but at last it had to go, and then I just gave up and put on a linsey-woolsey gown. When a girl's spirit's once broke, she don't care for nothing, you know; so, when the Community offered to take Sol back as coal-digger, I just said, "Go," and we come.' Here she tried to smear the tears away with her bony hands, and gave a low groan.

'Groaning probably relieves you,' observed Ermine.

'Yes, 'm. It's kinder company like, when I'm all alone. But you see it's hard on the prettiest girl in Sandy to have to live in this lone lorn place. Why, ladies, you mightn't believe it, but I had open-work stockings, and feathers in my winter bunnets before I was married!' And the tears broke forth afresh.

'Accept my handkerchief,' said Ermine; 'it will serve your purpose better than fingers.'

The woman took the dainty cambric and surveyed it curiously, held at arm's length. 'Reg'lar thistle-down, now, ain't it?' she said; 'and smells like a locust-tree blossom.'

'Mr Solomon, then, belonged to the Community?' I asked, trying to gather up the threads of the story.

'No he didn't either; he's no Dutchman, I reckon, he's a Lake County man, born near Painesville, he is.'

'I thought you spoke as though he had been in the Community.'

'So he had; he didn't belong, but he worked for 'em since he was a boy, did middling well, in spite of the painting, until one day, when he come over to Sandy on a load of wood and seen me standing at the door. That was the end of him,' continued the woman, with an air of girlish pride; 'he couldn't work no more for thinking of me.'

'Où la vanité va-t-elle se nicher?' murmured Ermine, rising. 'Come, Dora, it is time to return.'

As I hastily finished my last cup of sulphur water, our hostess followed Ermine towards the door. 'Will you have your handkercher back, marm?' she said, holding it out reluctantly.

'It was a free gift, madam,' replied my cousin; 'I wish you a good afternoon.'

'Say, will yer be coming again to-morrow?' asked the woman as I took my departure.

'Very likely; good by.'

The door closed, and then, but not till then, the melancholy dog joined us and stalked behind until we had crossed the meadow and reached the gate. We passed out and turned up the hill; but looking back we saw the outline of the woman's head at the upper window, and the dog's head at the bars, both watching us out of sight.

In the evening there came a cold wind down from the north, and the parlor, with its primitive ventilators, square openings in the side of the house, grew chilly. So a great fire of soft coal was built in the broad Franklin stove, and before its blaze we made good cheer, nor needed the one candle which flickered on the table behind us. Cider fresh from the mill, carded ginger-bread, and new cheese crowned the scene, and during the evening came a band of singers, the young people of the Community, and sang for us the song of the Lorelei, accompanied by home-made violins and flageolets. At length we were left alone, the candle had burned out, the house door was barred, and the peaceful Community was asleep; still we two sat together with our feet upon the hearth, looking down into the glowing coals.

'Ich weisz nicht was soll es bedeuten
Dasz ich so traurig bin,'

I said, repeating the opening lines of the Lorelei; 'I feel absolutely blue to-night.'

'The memory of the sulphur-woman,' suggested Ermine.

'Sulphur-woman! What a name!'

'Entirely appropriate, in my opinion.'

'Poor thing! How she longed with a great longing for the finery of her youth in Sandy.'

'I suppose from those barbarous pictures that she was originally in the flesh,' mused Ermine; 'at present she is but a bony outline.'

'Such as she is, however, she has had her romance,' I answered. 'She is quite sure that there was one to love her; then let come what may, she has had her day.'

'Misquoting Tennyson on such a subject!' said Ermine, with disdain.

'A man's a man for all that and a woman's a woman too,' I retorted. 'You are blind, cousin, blinded with pride. That woman has had her tragedy, as real and bitter as any that can come to us.'

'What have you to say for the poor man, then!' exclaimed Ermine, rousing to the contest. 'If there is a tragedy at the sulphur-house, it belongs to the sulphur-man, not to the sulphur-woman.'

'He is not a sulphur-man, he is a coal-man; keep to your bearings, Ermine.'

'I tell you,' pursued my cousin, earnestly, 'that I pitied that unknown man with inward tears all the while I sat by that trap door. Depend upon it, he had his dream, his ideal; and this country girl with her great eyes and wealth of hair represented the beautiful to his hungry soul. He gave his whole life and hope into her hands, and woke to find his goddess a common wooden image.'

'Waste sympathy upon a coal-miner!' I said, imitating my cousin's former tone.

'If any one is blind, it is you,' she answered, with gleaming eyes. 'That man's whole history stood revealed in the selfish complainings of that creature. He had been in the Community from boyhood, therefore of course he had no chance to learn life, to see its art-treasures. He has been shipwrecked, poor soul; hopelessly shipwrecked.'

'She too, Ermine.'

'She!'

'Yes. If he loved pictures, she loved her chany and her feather-beds, not to speak of the big looking-glass. No doubt she had other lovers, and might have lived in a red brick farmhouse with ten unopened front windows and a blistered front door. The wives of men of genius are always to be pitied; they do not soar into the crowd of feminine admirers who circle round the husband, and they are therefore called 'grubs,' 'worms of the earth,' 'drudges,' and other sweet titles.'

'Nonsense,' said Ermine, tumbling the arched coals into chaos with the poker; 'it's after midnight, let us go up stairs.' I knew very well that my beautiful cousin enjoyed the society of several poets, painters, musicians, and others of that ilk, without concerning herself about their stay-at-home wives.

The next day the winds were out in battle array, howling over the Strasburg hill, raging up and down the river, and whirling the colored leaves wildly along the lovely road to the One-Leg Creek. Evidently there could be no rambling in the painted woods that day, so we went over to old Fritz's shop, played on his home-made piano, inspected the woolly horse who turned his crank patiently in an underground den, and set in motion all the curious little images which the carpenter's deft fingers had wrought. Fritz belonged to the Community, and knew nothing of the outside world; he had a taste for mechanism, which showed itself in many labor-saving devices, and with it all he was the roundest, kindest little man, with bright eyes like a canary-bird.

'Do you know Solomon the coal-miner?' asked Ermine, in her correct, well-learned German.

'Sol Bangs? Yes, I know him,' replied Fritz in his Würtemburg dialect.

'What kind of a man is he?'

'Good for nothing,' replied Fritz, placidly.

'Why?'

'Wrong here'; tapping his forehead.

'Do you know his wife?' I asked.

'Yes.'

'What kind of a woman is she?'

'Too much tongue. Women must not talk much.'

'Old Fritz touched us both there,' I said, as we ran back laughing to the hotel through the blustering wind. 'In his opinion, I suppose, we have the popular verdict of the township upon our two *protégés*, the sulphur-woman and her husband.'

The next day opened calm, hazy, and warm, the perfection of Indian summer; the breezy hill was outlined in purple, and the trees glowed in rich colors. In the afternoon we started for the sulphur-spring without shawls or wraps, for the heat was almost oppressive; we loitered on the way through the still woods, gathering the tinted leaves, and wondering why no poet has yet arisen to celebrate in fit words the glories of the American autumn. At last we reached the turn whence the lonely house came into view, and at the bars we saw the dog awaiting us.

'Evidently the sulphur-woman does not like that melancholy animal,' I said, as we applied our united strength to the gate.

'Did you ever know a woman of limited mind who liked a large dog?' replied Ermine. 'Occasionally such a woman will fancy a small cur; but to appreciate a large, noble dog requires a large, noble mind.'

'Nonsense with your dogs and minds,' I said, laughing, 'Wonderful! There is a curtain.'

It was true. The paper had been removed from one of the windows, and in its place hung some white drapery, probably part of a sheet rigged as a curtain.

Before we reached the piazza the door opened, and our hostess appeared. 'Glad to see yer, ladies,' she said. 'Walk right in this way to the keeping room.'

The dog went away to his block-house, and we followed the woman into a room on the right of the hall; there were three rooms, beside the attic above. An Old-World German stove of brick-work occupied a large portion of the space, and over it hung a few tins, and a clock whose pendulum swung outside; a table, a settle, and some stools completed the furniture; but on the plastered walls were two rude brackets, one holding a cup and saucer of figured china, and the other surmounted by a large bunch of autumn leaves, so beautiful in themselves and so exquisitely arranged that we crossed the room to admire them.

'Sol fixed 'em, he did,' said the sulphur-woman; 'he seen me setting things to rights, and he would do it. I told him they was trash, but he made me promise to leave 'em alone in case you should call again.'

'Madam Bangs, they would adorn a palace,' said Ermine, severely.

'The cup is pretty too,' I observed, seeing the woman's eyes turn that way.

'It's the last of my chany' she answered, with pathos in her voice,—'the very last piece.'

As we took our places on the settle we noticed the brave attire of our hostess. The delaine was there; but how altered! Flounces it had, skimped, but still flounces, and at the top was a collar of crochet cotton reaching nearly to the shoulders; the hair, too, was braided in imitation of Ermine's sunny coronet, and the Roman scarf did duty as a belt around the large flat waist.

'You see she tries to improve,' I whispered, as Mrs. Bangs went into the hall to get some sulphur-water for us.

'Vanity,' answered Ermine.

We drank our dose slowly, and our hostess talked on and on. Even I, her champion, began to weary of her complainings. 'How dark it is!' said Ermine at last, rising and drawing aside the curtain. 'See, Dora, a storm is close upon us.'

We hurried to the door, but one look at the black cloud was enough to convince us that we could not reach the Community hotel before it would break, and somewhat drearily we returned to the keeping-room, which grew darker and darker, until our hostess was obliged to light a candle. 'Reckon you'll have to stay all night; I'd like to have you ladies,' she said. 'The Community ain't got nothing covered to send after you, except the old king's coach, and I misdoubt they won't let that out in such a storm, steps and all. When it begins to rain in this valley, it do rain, I can tell you; and from the way it's begun, 't won't stop 'fore morning. You just let me send the Roarer over to the mine, he'll tell Sol; Sol can tell the Community folks, so they'll know where you be.'

I looked somewhat aghast at this proposal, but Ermine listened to the rain upon the roof a moment, and then quietly accepted; she remembered the long hills of tenacious red clay and her kid boots were dear to her.

'The Roarer, I presume, is some faithful kobold who bears your message to and from the mine,' she said, making herself as comfortable as the wooden settle would allow.

The sulphur-woman stared. 'Roarer's Sol's old dog,' she answered, opening the door; perhaps one of you will write a bit of a note for him to carry in his basket,—Roarer, Roarer!'

The melancholy dog came slowly in, and stood still while she tied a small covered basket around his neck.

Ermine took a leaf from her tablets and wrote a line or two with the gold pencil attached to her watch-chain.

'Well now, you do have everything handy, I do declare,' said the woman, admiringly.

I glanced at the paper.

'MR. SOLOMON BANGS: My cousin Theodora Wentworth and myself have accepted the hospitality of your house for the night. Will you be so good as to send tidings of our safety to the Community, and oblige,

ERMINIA STUART.'

The Roarer started obediently out into the rain-storm with his little basket; he did not run, but walked slowly, as if the storm was nothing compared to his settled melancholy.

'What a note to send to a coal-miner!' I said, during a momentary absence of our hostess.

'Never fear; it will be appreciated,' replied Ermine.

'What is this king's carriage of which you spoke?' I asked, during the next hour's conversation.

'O, when they first come over from Germany, they had a sort of a king; he knew more than the rest, and he lived in that big brick house with dormel-winders and a cuperler, that stands next the garden. The carriage was hisn, and it had steps to let down, and curtains and all; they don't use it much now he's dead. They're a queer set anyhow! The women look like meal-sacks. After Sol seen me, he couldn't abide to look at 'em.'

Soon after six we heard the great gate creak.

'That's Sol,' said the woman,' and now of course Roarer'll come in and track all over my floor.' The hall door opened and a shadow passed into the opposite room, two shadows,—a man and a dog.

'He's going to wash himself now,' continued the wife; 'he's always washing himself, just like a horse.'

'New fact in natural history, Dora love,' observed Ermine.

After some moments the miner appeared,—a tall, stooping figure with high forehead, large blue eyes, and long thin yellow hair; there was a singularly lifeless expression in his face, and a far-off look in his eyes. He gazed about the room in an absent way, as though he scarcely saw us. Behind him stalked the Roarer, wagging his tail slowly from side to side.

'Now, then, dont yer see the ladies, Sol? Where's yer manners?' said his wife, sharply.

'Ah,—yes,—good evening,' he said, vaguely. Then his wandering eyes fell upon Ermine's beautiful face, and fixed themselves there with strange intentness.

'You received my note, Mr. Bangs?' said my cousin in her soft voice.

'Yes, surely. You are Erminia,' replied the man, still standing in the centre of the room with fixed eyes. The Roarer laid himself down behind his master, and his tail still wagging, sounded upon the floor with a regular tap.

'Now then, Sol, since you've come home, perhaps you'll entertain the ladies while I get supper,' quoth Mrs. Bangs; and forthwith began a clatter of pans.

The man passed his long hand abstractedly over his forehead. 'Eh,' he said with long-drawn utterance,—'eh-h? Yes, my rose of Sharon, certainly, certainly.'

'Then why don't you do it!' said the woman, lighting the fire in the brick stove.

'And what will the ladies please to do?' he answered, his eyes going back to Ermine.

'We will look over your pictures, sir,' said my cousin, rising; 'they are in the upper room, I believe.'

A great flush rose in the painter's thin cheeks. 'Will you,' he said eagerly,—'will you? Come!'

'It's a broken-down old hole, ladies; Sol will never let me sweep it out. Reckon you'll be more comfortable here,' said Mrs. Bangs, with her arms in the flour.

'No, no, my lily of the valley. The ladies will come with me; they will not scorn the poor room.'

'A studio is always interesting,' said Ermine, sweeping up the rough stairs behind Solomon's candle. The dog followed us, and laid himself down on an old mat, as though well accustomed to the place. 'Eh-h, boy, you came bravely through the storm with the lady's note.' said his master, beginning to light candle after candle. 'See him laugh!'

'Can a dog laugh?'

'Certainly; look at him now. What is that but a grin of happy contentment? Don't the Bible say, "grin like a dog"?'

'You seem much attached to the Roarer.'

'Tuscarora, lady, Tuscarora. Yes, I love him well. He has been with me through all, he has watched the making of all my pictures; he always lies there when I paint.'

By this time a dozen candles were burning on shelves and brackets, and we could see all parts of the attic studio. It was but a poor place, unfloored in the corners where the roof slanted down, and having no ceiling but the dark beams and thatch; hung upon the walls were the pictures we had seen, and many others, all crude and high colored, and all representing the same face,—the sulphur-woman in her youth, the poor artist's only ideal. He showed us these one by one, handling them tenderly, and telling us, in his quaint language, all they symbolized. 'This is Ruth, and denoteth the power of hope,' he said. 'Behold Judith, the queen of revenge. And this dear one is Rachel, for whom Jacob served seven years, and they seemed unto him but a day, so well he loved her.' The light shone on his pale face, and we noticed the far-off look in his eyes, and the long, tapering fingers coming out from the hard-worked broad palm. To me it was a melancholy scene, the poor artist with his daubs and the dreary attic.

But Ermine seemed eagerly interested; she looked at the staring pictures, listened to the explanations, and at last she said gently, 'Let me show you something of perspective, and the part that shadows play in a pictured face. Have you any crayons?'

No; the man had only his coarse paints and lumps of charcoal; taking a piece of the coal in her delicate hand, my cousin began to work upon a sheet of drawing-paper attached to the rough easel. Solomon watched her intently, as she explained and demonstrated some of the rules of drawing, the lights and shades, and the manner of representing the different features and curves. All his pictures were full faces, flat and unshaded; Ermine showed him the power of the profile and the three-quarter view. I grew weary of watching them, and pressing my face against the little window gazed out into the night; steadily the rain came down and the hills shut us in like a well. I thought of our home in C—, and its bright lights, warmth, company, and life. Why should we come masquerading out among the Ohio hills at this late season? And then I remembered that it was because Ermine would come; she liked such expeditions, and from childhood I had always followed her lead. '*Dux nascitur*, etc., etc.' Turning away from the gloomy night, I looked towards the easel again; Solomon's cheeks were deeply flushed, and his eyes shone like stars. The lesson went on, the merely mechanical hand explaining its art to the ignorant fingers of genius. Ermine had taken lessons all her life, but she had never produced an original picture, only copies.

At last the lesson was interrupted by a voice from below, 'Sol, Sol, supper's ready!' No one stirred until, feeling some sympathy for the amount of work which my ears told me had been going on below, I woke up the two enthusiasts and took them away from the easel down stairs into the keeping-room, where a loaded table and a scarlet hostess bore witness to the truth of my surmise. Strange things we ate that night, dishes unheard of in towns, but not unpalatable. Ermine had the one china cup for her corn-coffee; her grand air always secured her such favors. Tuscarora was there and ate of the best, now and then laying his shaggy head on the table, and, as his master said, 'smiling at us'; evidently the evening was his gala time. It was nearly nine when the feast was ended, and I immediately proposed retiring to bed, for, having but little art enthusiasm, I dreaded a vigil in that dreary attic. Solomon looked disappointed, but I ruthlessly carried off Ermine to the opposite room, which we afterwards suspected was the apartment of our hosts, freshened and set in order in our honor. The sound of the rain on the piazza roof lulled us soon to sleep, in spite of the strange surroundings; but more than once I woke and wondered where I was, suddenly remembering the lonely house in its lonely valley with a shiver of discomfort. The next morning we woke at our usual hour, but some time after the miner's departure; breakfast was awaiting us in the keeping-room, and our hostess said that an ox-team from the Community would come for us before nine.

She seemed sorry to part with us, and refused any remuneration for our stay; but none the less did we promise ourselves to send some dresses and even ornaments from C—, to feed that poor, starving love of finery. As we rode away in the ox-cart, the Roarer looked wistfully after us through the bars; but his melancholy mood was upon him again, and he had not the heart even to wag his tail.

As we were sitting in the hotel parlor, in front of our soft-coal fire in the evening of the following day, and discussing whether or no we should return to the city within the week, the old landlord entered without his broad-brimmed hat,—an unusual attention, since he was a trustee and a man of note in the Community, and removed his hat for no one or nothing; we even suspected that he slept in it.

'You know Zolomon Barngs,' he said, slowly.

'Yes,' we answered.

'Well, he's dead. Kilt in de mine.' And putting on the hat, removed, we now saw, in respect for death, he left the room suddenly as he had entered it. As it happened, we had been discussing the couple, I, as usual, contending for the wife, and Ermine, as usual, advocating the cause of the husband.

'Let us go out there immediately to see her, poor woman!' I said, rising.

'Yes, poor man, we will go to him!' said Ermine.

'But the man is dead, cousin.'

'Then he shall at least have one kind friendly glance before he is carried to his grave,' answered Ermine quietly.

In a short time we set out in the darkness, and dearly did we have to pay for the night-ride; no one could understand the motive of our going, but money was money, and we could pay for all peculiarities. It was a dark night, and the ride seemed endless as the oxen moved slowly on through the red-clay mire. At last we reached the turn and saw the little lonely house with its upper room brightly lighted.

'He is in the studio,' said Ermine; and so it proved. He was not dead, but dying; not maimed but poisoned by the gas of the mine, and rescued too late for recovery. They had placed him upon the floor on a couch of blankets and the dull-eyed Community doctor stood at his side. 'No good, no good,' he said; 'he must die.' And then, hearing of the returning cart, he left us, and we could hear the tramp of the oxen over the little bridge, on their way back to the village.

The dying man's head lay upon his wife's breast, and her arms supported him; she did not speak, but gazed at us with a dumb agony in her large eyes. Ermine knelt down and took the lifeless hand streaked with coal-dust in both her own. 'Solomon,' she said, in her soft, clear voice, 'do you know me?'

The closed eyes opened slowly, and fixed themselves upon her face a moment: then they turned towards the window, as if seeking something.

'It's the picter he means,' said the wife. 'He sat up most all last night a doing it.'

I lighted all the candles, and Ermine brought forward the easel; upon it stood a sketch in charcoal wonderful to behold,—the same face, the face of the faded wife, but so noble in its idealized beauty that it might have been a portrait of her glorified face in Paradise. It was a profile, with the eyes upturned,—a mere outline, but grand in conception and expression. I gazed in silent astonishment.

Ermine said, 'Yes, I knew you could do it, Solomon. It is perfect of its kind.' The shadow of a smile stole over the pallid face, and then the husband's fading gaze turned upward to meet the wild, dark eyes of the wife.

'It's you, Dorcas,' he murmured; 'that's how you looked to me, but I never could get it right before.' She bent over him, and silently we watched the coming of the shadow of death; he spoke only once, 'My rose of Sharon—' And then in a moment he was gone, the poor artist was dead.

Wild, wild was the grief of the ungoverned heart left behind; she was like a mad-woman, and our united strength was needed to keep her from injuring herself in her frenzy. I was frightened, but Ermine's strong little hands and lithe arms kept her down until, exhausted, she lay motionless near her dead husband. Then we carried her down stairs and I watched by the bedside, while my cousin went back to the studio. She was absent some time, and then she came back to keep the vigil with me through the long, still night. At dawn the woman woke, and her face looked aged in the gray light. She was quiet, and took without a word the food we had prepared awkwardly enough, in the keeping-room.

'I must go to him, I must go to him.' she murmured, as we led her back.

'Yes,' said Ermine, 'but first let me make you tidy. He loved to see you neat.' And with deft, gentle touch she dressed the poor creature, arranging the heavy hair so artistically that, for the first time, I saw what she might have been, and understood the husband's dream.

'What is that?' I said, as a peculiar sound startled us.

'It's Roarer. He was tied up last night, but I suppose he's gnawed the rope,' said the woman. I opened the hall door, and in stalked the great dog, smelling his way directly up the stairs.

'O, he must not go!' I exclaimed.

'Yes, let him go, he loved his master,' said Ermine; 'we will go too.' So silently we all went up into the chamber of death.

The pictures had been taken down from the walls, but the wonderful sketch remained on the easel, which had been moved to the head of the couch where Solomon lay. His long, light hair was smooth, his face peacefully quiet, and on his breast lay the beautiful bunch of autumn leaves which he had arranged in our honor. It was a striking picture,—the noble face of the sketch above, and the dead face of the artist below. It brought to my mind a design I had once seen, where Fame with her laurels came at last to the door of the poor artist and gently knocked; but he had died the night before!

The dog lay at his master's feet, nor stirred until Solomon was carried out to his grave.

The Community buried the miner in one corner of the lonely little meadow. No service had they and no mound was raised to mark the spot, for such was their custom; but in the early spring we went down again into the valley, and placed a block of granite over the grave. It bore the inscription:—

SOLOMON

He will finish his work in heaven.

Strange as it may seem, the wife pined for her artist husband. We found her in the Community trying to work, but so aged and bent that we hardly knew her. Her large eyes had lost their peevish discontent, and a great sadness had taken the place.

'Seems like I couldn't get on without Sol,' she said, sitting with us in the hotel parlor after work-hours. 'I kinder miss his voice and all them names he used to call me; he got 'em out of the Bible, so they must have been good, you know. He always thought everything I did was right, and he thought no end of my good looks, too; I suppose I've lost 'em all now. He was mighty fond of me; nobody in all the world cares a straw for me now. Even Roarer wouldn't stay with me, for all I petted him; he kep' a going out to that meader and a lying by Sol, until, one day, we found him there dead. He just died of sheer loneliness, I reckon. I sha'n't have to stop long I know, because I keep a dreaming of Sol, and he always looks at me like he did when I first knew him. He was a beautiful boy when I first saw him on that load of wood coming into Sandy. Well, ladies, I must go. Thank you kindly for all you've done for me. And say, Miss Stuart, when I die you shall have that coal pictur; no one else 'ud vally it so much.'

Three months after, while we were at the sea-shore, Ermine received a long tin case, directed in a peculiar handwriting; it had been forwarded from C—, and contained the sketch and a note from the Community.

'E. STUART: The woman Dorcas Bangs died this day. She will be put away by the side of her husband, Solomon Bangs. She left the enclosed picture, which we hereby send, and which please acknowledge by return of mail.

'JACOB BOLL, *Trustee*.'

I unfolded the wrappings and looked at the sketch; 'It is indeed striking,' I said. 'She must have been beautiful once, poor woman!'

'Let us hope that at least she is beautiful now, for her husband's sake poor man!' replied Ermine.

Even then we could not give up our preferences.

WILHELMINA

'AND so, Mina, you will not marry the baker?'

'No: I waits for Gustav.'

'How long is it since you have seen him?'

'Three year; it was a three-year regi-mènt.'

'Then he will soon be home?'

'I not know' answered the girl, with a wistful look in her dark eyes, as if asking information from the superior being who sat in the skiff,—a being from the outside world where newspapers, the modern Tree of Knowledge, were not forbidden.

'Perhaps he will re-enlist, and stay three years longer,' I said.

'Ah, lady,—six year! It breaks the heart,' answered Wilhelmina.

She was the gardener's daughter, a member of the Community of German Separatists who live secluded in one of Ohio's rich valleys, separated by their own broad acres and orchard-covered hills from the busy world outside; down the valley flows the tranquil Tuscarawas on its way to the Muskingum, its slow tide rolling through the fertile bottom-lands between stone dikes, and utilized to the utmost extent of carefulness by the thrifty brothers, now working a saw-mill on the bank, now sending a tributary to the flour-mill across the canal, and now branching off in a sparkling race across the valley to turn wheels for two or three factories, watering the great grass meadow on the way. We were floating on this river in a skiff named by myself Der Fliegende Holländer, much to the slow wonder of the Zoarites, who did not understand how a Dutchman could, nor why he should, fly. Wilhelmina sat before me, her oars trailing in the water. She showed a Nubian head above her white kerchief: large-lidded soft brown eyes, heavy braids of dark hair, creamy skin with, purple tints in the lips and brown shadows under the eyes, and a far off expression which even the steady monotonous toil of Community life had not been able to efface. She wore the blue dress and white kerchief of the society, the quaint little calico bonnet lying beside her; she was a small maiden; her slender form swayed in the stiff, short-waisted gown, her feet slipped about in the broad shoes, and her hands, roughened and browned with garden-work, were yet narrow and graceful. From the first we felt sure she was grafted, and not a shoot from the Community stalk. But we could learn nothing of her origin; the Zoarites are not communicative; they fill each day with twelve good hours of labor, and look neither forward nor back. 'She is a daughter,' said the old gardener in answer to our questions. 'Adopted?' I suggested; but he vouchsafed no answer. I liked the little daughter's dreamy face, but she was pale and undeveloped, like a Southern flower growing in Northern soil; the rosy-cheeked, flaxen-haired Rosines, Salomes, and Dorotys, with their broad shoulders and ponderous tread, thought this brown changeling ugly, and pitied her in their slow, good-natured way.

'It breaks the heart,' said Wilhelmina again, softly, as if to herself.

I repented me of my thoughtlessness. 'In any case he can come back for a few days,' I hastened to say. 'What regiment was it?'

'The One Hundred and Seventh, lady.'

I had a Cleveland paper in my basket, and taking it out I glanced over the war-news column, carelessly, as one who does not expect to find what he seeks. But chance was with us and gave this item: 'The One Hundred and Seventh Regiment, O. V. I., is expected home next week. The men will be paid off at Camp Chase.'

'Ah!' said Wilhelmina, catching her breath with a half-sob under her tightly drawn kerchief—'ah, mein Gustav!'

'Yes, you will soon see him,' I answered, bending forward to take the rough little hand in mine; for I was a romantic wife, and my heart went out to all lovers. But the girl did not notice my words or my touch; silently she sat, absorbed in her own emotion, her eyes fixed on the hilltops far away, as though she saw the regiment marching home through the blue June sky.

I took the oars and rowed up as far as the inland, letting the skiff float back with the current. Other boats were out, filled with fresh-faced boys in their high-crowned hats, long-waisted, wide-flapped vests of calico, and funny little swallow-tailed coats with buttons up under the shoulder-blades; they appeared unaccountably long in front, and short behind, these young Zoar brethren. On the vine-covered dike were groups of mothers and grave little children, and up in the hill-orchards were moving figures, young and old; the whole village was abroad in the lovely afternoon, according to their Sunday custom, which gave the morning to chorals and a long sermon in the little church, and the afternoon to nature, even old Christian, the pastor, taking his imposing white fur hat and tasselled cane for a walk through the

Community fields, with the remark, 'Thus is cheered the heart of man, and his countenance refreshed.'

As the sun sank in the, warm western sky, homeward came the villagers from the river, the orchards, and the meadows, men, women and children, a hardy, simple-minded band, whose fathers, for religion's sake, had taken the long journey from Würtemburg across the ocean to this distant valley, and made it a garden of rest in the wilderness. We, too, landed, and walked up the apple-tree lane towards the hotel.

'The cows come,' said Wilhelmina as we heard a distant, tinkling; 'I must go.' But still she lingered. 'Der regi-mènt, it come soon, you say?' she asked in a low voice, as though she wanted to hear the good news again and again.

'They will be paid off next week; they cannot be later than ten days from now.'

'Ten day? Ah, mein Gustav,' murmured the little maiden; she turned away and tied on her stiff bonnet, furtively wiping off a tear with her prim handkerchief folded in a square.

'Why, my child,' I said, following her and stooping to look in her face, 'what is this?'

'It is nothing; it is for glad,—for very glad,' said Wilhelmina. Away she ran as the first solemn cow came into view, heading the long procession meandering slowly towards the stalls. They knew nothing of haste, these dignified Community cows; from stall to pasture, from pasture to stall, in a plethora of comfort, this was their life. The silver-haired shepherd came last with his staff and scrip, and the nervous shepherd-dog ran hither and thither in the hope of finding some cow to bark at, but the comfortable cows moved on in orderly ranks, and he was obliged to dart off on a tangent every now and then, and bark at nothing, to relieve his feelings. Reaching the paved court-yard each cow walked into her own stall, and the milking began. All the girls took part in this work, sitting on little stools and singing together as the milk frothed up in the tin pails; the pails were emptied into tubs, and when the tubs were full the girls bore them on their heads to the dairy, where the milk was poured into a huge strainer, a constant procession of girls with tubs above and the old milk-mother ladling out as fast as she could below. With the beehives near by, it was a realization of the Scriptural phrase, 'A land flowing with milk and honey.'

The next morning, after breakfast, I strolled up the still street, leaving the Wirthshaus with its pointed roof behind me. On the right were some ancient cottages built of crossed timbers filled in with plaster; sundials hung on the walls, and each house had its piazza, where, when the work of the day was over, the families assembled, often singing folk-songs to the music of their home-made flutes and pipes. On the left stood the residence of the first pastor, the reverend man who had led these sheep to their refuge in the wilds of the New World. It was a wide-spreading brick mansion, with a broadside of white-curtained windows, an enclosed glass porch, iron railings, and gilded eaves; a building so stately among the surrounding cottages, it had gained from outsiders the name of the King's Palace, although the good man whose grave remains unmarked in the quiet God's Acre, according to the Separatist custom, was a father to his people, not a king.

Beyond the palace began the Community garden, a large square in the centre of the village filled with flowers and fruit adorned with arbors and cedar-trees clipped in the form of birds, and enriched with an old-style greenhouse whose sliding glasses were viewed with admiration by the visitors of thirty years ago, who sent their choice plants thither from far and near to be tended through the long, cold lake-country winters. The garden, the cedars, and the greenhouse were all antiquated, but to me none the less charming. The spring that gushed up in one corner, the old-fashioned flowers in their box-bordered beds, larkspur, lady slippers, bachelor's buttons, peonies, aromatic pinks, and all varieties of roses, the arbors with red honeysuckle overhead and tan bark under foot, were all delightful; and I knew, also, that I should find the gardener's daughter at her never-ending task of weeding. This time it was the strawberry bed. 'I have come to sit in your pleasant garden, Mina,' I said, taking a seat on a shaded bench near the bending figure.

'So?' said Wilhelmina in long-drawn interrogation, glancing up shyly with a smile. She was a child of the sun, this little maiden, and while her blond companions wore always their bonnets or broad-brimmed hats over their precise caps, Wilhelmina, as now, constantly discarded these coverings and sat in the sun basking like a bird of the tropics. In truth, it did not redden her; she was one of those whose coloring comes not from without, but within.

'Do you like this work, Mina?'

'O—so. Good as any.'

'Do you like work?'

'Folks must work.' This was, said gravely, as part of the Community creed.

'Wouldn't you like to go with me to the city?'

'No; I's better here.'

'But you can see the great world, Mina. You need not work, I will take care of you. You shall have pretty dresses; wouldn't you like that?' I asked, curious to discover the secret of the Separatist indifference to everything outside.

'Nein,' answered the little maiden, tranquilly; 'nein, fräulein. Ich bin zufrieden.'

Those three words were the key. 'I am contented.' So were they taught from childhood, and—I was about to say—they knew no better; but, after all, is there anything better to know?

We talked on, for Mina understood English, although many of her mates could chatter only in their Würtemberg dialect, whose provincialisms confused my carefully learned German; I was grounded in Goethe, well read in Schiller, and struggling with Jean Paul, who, fortunately, is 'der Einzige,' the only; another such would destroy life. At length a bell sounded, and forthwith work was laid aside in the fields, the workshops, and the houses, while all partook of a light repast, one of the five meals with which the long summer day of toil is broken. Flagons of beer had the men afield, with bread and cheese; the women took bread and apple-butter. But Mina did not care for the thick slice which the thrifty house-mother had provided; she had not the steady unfanciful appetite of the Community which eats the same food day after day, as the cow eats its grass, desiring no change.

'And the gardener really wishes you to marry Jacob?' I said as she sat on the grass near me, enjoying the rest.

'Yes, Jacob is good,—always the same.'

'And Gustav?'

'Ah, mein Gustav! Lady, *he* is young, tall,—so tall as tree; he run, he sing, his eyes like veilchen there, his hair like gold. If I see him not soon, lady, I die! The year so long,—so long they are. Three year without Gustav!' The brown eyes grew dim, and out came the square-folded handkerchief, of colored calico for week-days.

'But it will not be long now, Mina.'

'Yes; I hope.'

'He writes to you, I suppose?'

'No. Gustav knows not to write, he not like school. But he speak through the other boys, Ernst the verliebte of Rosine, and Peter of Doroty.'

'The Zoar soldiers were all young men?'

'Yes; all verliebte. Some are not; they have gone to the Next Country' (died).

'Killed in Battle?'

'Yes; on the berge that looks,—what you call I not know.'

'Lookout Mountain?'

'Yes'

'Were the boys volunteers?' I asked, remembering the Community theory of non-resistance.

'O yes; they volunteer, Gustav the first. *They* not drafted,' said Wilhelmina, proudly. For these two words so prominent during the war, had penetrated even into this quiet little valley.

'But did the trustees approve?'

'Apperouve?'

'I mean did they like it?'

'Ah! they like it not. They talk, they preach in church, they say 'No.' Zoar must give soldiers? So. Then they take money and pay for der substitute; but the boys they must not go.'

'But they went in spite of the trustees?'

'Yes; Gustav first. They go in night, they walk in woods, over the hills to Brownville, where is der recruiter. The morning come, they gone!'

'They have been away three years, you say? They have seen the world in that time,' I remarked half to myself, as I thought of the strange mind-opening and knowledge-gaining of those years to youths brought up in the strict seclusion of the Community.

'Yes; Gustav have seen the wide world,' answered Wilhelmina with pride.

'But will they be content to step back into the dull routine of Zoar life?' I thought; and a doubt came that made me scan more closely the face of the girl at my side. To me it was attractive because of its possibilities; I was always fancying some excitement that would bring the color to the cheeks and full lips, and light up the heavy-lidded eyes with soft brilliancy. But would this Gustav see these might-be beauties? And how far would the singularly ugly costume offend eyes grown accustomed to fanciful finery and gay colors?

'You fully expect to marry Gustav?' I asked.

'We are verlobt,' answered Mina, not without a little air of dignity.

'Yes, I know. But that was long ago.'

'Verlobt once, verlobt always,' said the little maiden, confidently.

'But why, then, does the gardener speak of Jacob, if you are engaged to this Gustav?'

'O, fader he like the old, and Jacob is old, thirty year! His wife is gone to the Next Country. Jacob is a brother, too; he write his name in the book. But Gustav he not do so; he is free.'

'You mean that the baker has signed the articles, and is a member of the Community?'

'Yes; but the baker is old, very old; thirty year! Gustav not twenty and three yet; he come home, then he sign.'

'And have you signed these articles, Wilhelmina?'

'Yes; all the womens signs.'

'What does the paper say?'

'Da ich Unterzeichneter,'—began the girl.

'I cannot understand that. Tell me in English.'

'Well; you wants to join the Zoar Community of Separatists; you writes your name and says, "Give me house, victual, and clothes for my work and I join; and I never fernerer Forderung an besagte Gesellschaft machen kann, oder will."'

'Will never make further demand upon said society,' I repeated, translating slowly.

'Yes; that is it.'

'But who takes charge of all the money?'

'The trustees.'

'Don't they give you any?'

'No; for what? It's no good,' answered Wilhelmina.

I knew that all the necessaries of life were dealt out to the members of the Community according to their need, and, as they never went outside of their valley, they could scarcely have spent money even if they had possessed it. But, nevertheless, it was startling in this nineteenth century to come upon a sincere belief in the worthlessness of the green-tinted paper we cherish so fondly. 'Gustav will have learned its value,' I thought, as Mina, having finished the strawberry-bed, started away towards the dairy to assist in the butter-making.

I strolled on up the little hill, past the picturesque bakery, where through the open window I caught a glimpse of the 'old, very old Jacob,' a serious young man of thirty, drawing out his large loaves of bread from the brick oven with a long-handled rake. It was gingerbread-day also, and a spicy odor met me at the window; so I put in my head and asked for a piece, receiving a card about a foot square, laid on fresh grape-leaves.

'But I cannot eat all this,' I said, breaking off a corner.

'O, dat's noding!' answered Jacob, beginning to knead fresh dough in a long white trough, the village supply for the next day.

'I have been sitting with Wilhelmina,' I remarked, as I leaned on the casement, impelled by a desire to see the effect of the name.

'So?' said Jacob, interrogatively.

'Yes; she is a sweet girl.'

'So?' (doubtfully.)

'Dont you think so, Jacob?'

'Ye-es. So-so. A leetle black,' answered this impassive lover.

'But you wish to marry her?'

'O, ye-es. She young and strong; her fader say she good to work. I have children five; I must have some one in the house.'

'O Jacob! Is that the way to talk?' I exclaimed.

'Warum nicht?' replied the baker, pausing in his kneading, and regarding me with wide-open, candid eyes.

'Why not, indeed?' I thought, as I turned away from the window. 'He is at least honest, and no doubt in his way he would be a kind husband to little Mina. But what a way.'

I walked on up the street, passing the pleasant house where all the infirm old women of the Community were lodged together, carefully tended by appointed nurses. The aged sisters were out on the piazza sunning themselves, like so many old cats. They were bent with hard, out-door labor for they belonged to the early days when the wild forest covered the fields now so rich, and only a few log-cabins stood on the site of the tidy cottages and gardens of the present village. Some of them had taken the long journey on foot from Philadelphia westward, four hundred and fifty miles, in the depths of winter. Well might they rest from their labors and sit in the sunshine, poor old souls!

A few days later, my friendly newspaper mentioned the arrival of the German regiment at Camp Chase. 'They will probably be paid off in a day or two,' I thought, 'and another day may bring them here.' Eager to be the first to tell the good news to my little favorite, I hastened to the garden, and found her engaged, as usual, in weeding.

'Mina,' I said, 'I have something to tell you. The regiment is at Camp Chase; you will see Gustav soon, perhaps this week.'

And there, before my eyes, the transformation I had often fancied took place; the color rushed to the brown surface, the cheeks and lips glowed in vivid red, and the heavy eyes opened wide and shone like stars, with a brilliancy that astonished and even disturbed me. The statue had a soul at last; the beauty dormant had awakened. But for the fire of that soul would this expected Pygmalion suffice? Would the real prince fill his place in the long-cherished dreams of this beauty of the wood?

The girl had risen as I spoke, and now she stood erect, trembling with excitement, her hands clasped on her breast, breathing quickly and heavily as though an overweight of joy was pressing down on her heart; her eyes were fixed upon my face, but she saw me not. Strange was her gaze, like the gaze of one walking in sleep. Her sloping shoulders seemed to expand and chafe against the stuff gown as though they would burst their bonds; the blood glowed in her face and throat, and her lips quivered, not as though tears were coming, but from the fulness of unuttered speech. Her emotion resembled the intensest fire of fever, and yet it seemed natural; like noon in the tropics when the gorgeous flowers flame in the white, shadowless heat. Thus stood Wilhelmina, looking up into the sky with eyes that challenged the sun.

'Come here, child,' I said; 'come here and sit by me. We will talk about it.'

But she neither saw nor heard me. I drew her down on the bench at my side; she yielded unconsciously; her slender form throbbed, and pulses were beating under my hands wherever I touched her. 'Mina!' I said again. But she did not answer. Like an unfolding rose, she revealed her hidden, beautiful heart, as though a spirit had breathed upon the bud; silenced in the presence of this great love, I ceased speaking, and left her to herself. After a time single words fell from her lips, broken utterances of happiness. I was as nothing; she was absorbed in the One. 'Gustav! mein Gustav!' It was like the bird's note, oft repeated, ever the same. So isolated, so intense was her joy, that, as often happens, my mind took refuge in the opposite extreme of commonplace, and I found myself wondering whether she would be able to eat boiled beef and cabbage for dinner, or fill the soft-soap barrel for the laundry-women, later in the day.

All the morning I sat under the trees with Wilhelmina, who had forgotten her life-long tasks as completely as though they had never existed. I hated to leave her to the leather-colored wife of the old gardener, and lingered until the sharp voice came from the distant house-door, calling, 'Veel-hel-meeny,' as the twelve-o'clock bell summoned the Community to dinner. But as Mina rose and swept back the heavy braid that had fallen from the little ivory stick which confined them, I saw that she was armed *cap-à-pie* in that full happiness from which all weapons glance off harmless.

All the rest of the day she was like a thing possessed. I followed her to the hill-pasture, whither she had gone to mind the cows, and found her coiled up on the grass in the blaze of the afternoon sun, like a little salamander. She was lost in day dreams, and the decorous cows had a holiday for once in their sober lives, wandering beyond bounds at will, and even tasting the dissipations of the marsh, standing unheeded in the bog up to their sleek knees. Wilhelmina had not many words to give me; her English vocabulary was limited; she had never read a line of romance nor a verse of poetry. The nearest approach to either was the Community hymn-book, containing the Separatist hymns, of which the following lines are a specimen,

"Ruhe ist das beste Gut
Dasz man haben kann,"—

"Rest is the best good
That man can have,"—

and which embody the religious doctrine of the Zoar Brethren, although they think, apparently, that the labor of twelve hours each day is necessary to its enjoyment. The 'Ruhe,' however, refers more especially to their quiet seclusion away from the turmoil of the wicked world outside.

The second morning after this it was evident that an unusual excitement was abroad in the phlegmatic village. All the daily duties were fulfilled as usual at the Wirthshaus: Pauline went up to the bakery with her board, and returned with her load of bread and bretzels balanced on her head; Jacobina served our coffee with slow precision; and the broad-shouldered, young-faced Lydia patted and puffed up our mountain-high feather-beds with due care. The men went afield at the blast of the horn, the workshops were full and the mills running. But, nevertheless, all was not the same; the air seemed full of mystery; there were whisperings when two met, furtive signals, and an inward excitement glowing in the faces of men, women, and children, hitherto placid as their own sheep. 'They have heard the news,' I said, after watching the tailor's Gretchen and the blacksmith's Barbara stop to exchange a whisper behind the wood-house. Later in the day we learned that several letters from the absent soldier-boys had been received that morning, announcing their arrival on the evening train. The news had flown from one end of the village to the other; and although the well-drilled hands were all at work, hearts were stirring with the greatest excitement of a lifetime, since there was hardly a house where there was not one expected. Each large house often held a number of families, stowed away in little sets of chambers, with one dining-room in common.

Several times during the day we saw the three trustees conferring apart with anxious faces. The war had been a sore trouble to them, owing to their conscientious scruples against rendering military service. They had hoped to remain non-combatants. But the country was on fire with patriotism, and nothing less than a *bona fide* Separatist in United States uniform would quiet the surrounding towns, long jealous of the wealth of this foreign community, misunderstanding its tenets, and glowing with that zeal against 'sympathizers' which kept star-spangled banners flying over every suspected house. 'Hang out the flag!' was their cry, and they demanded that Zoar should hang out its soldiers, giving them to understand that if not voluntarily hung out, they would soon be involuntarily hung up! A draft was ordered, and then the young men of the society, who had long chafed against their bonds, broke loose, volunteered, and marched away, principles or no principles, trustees or no trustees. These bold hearts once gone, the village sank into quietude again. Their letters, however, were a source of anxiety, coming as they did from the vain outside world; and the old postmaster, autocrat though he was, hardly dared to suppress them. But he said, shaking his head, that they 'had fallen upon troublous times,' and handed each dangerous envelope out with a groan. But the soldiers were not skilled penmen; their letters, few and far between, at length stopped entirely. Time passed, and the very existence of the runaways had become a far-off problem to the wise men of the Community, absorbed in their slow calculations and cautious agriculture, when now, suddenly, it forced itself upon them face to face, and they were required to solve it in the twinkling of an eye. The bold hearts were coming back, full of knowledge of the outside world, almost every house would hold one, and the bands of law and order would be broken. Before this prospect the trustees quailed. Twenty years before they would have forbidden the entrance of these unruly sons within their borders; but now they dared not, since even into Zoar had penetrated the knowledge that America was a free country. The younger generation were not as their fathers were; objections had been openly made to the cut of the Sunday coats, and the girls had spoken together of ribbons!

The shadows of twilight seemed very long in falling that night, but at last there was no further excuse for delaying the evening bell, and home came the laborers to their evening meal. There was no moon, a soft mist obscured the stars, and the night was darkened with the excess of richness which rose from the ripening valley-fields and fat bottom-lands along the river. The Community store opposite the Wirthshaus was closed early in the evening, the houses of the trustees were dark, and indeed the village was almost unlighted, as if to hide its own excitement. The entire population was abroad in the night, and one by one the men and boys stole away down the station road, a lovely, winding track on the hillside, following the river on its way down the valley to the little station on the grass-grown railroad, a branch from the main track. As ten o'clock came, the women and girls, grown bold with excitement, gathered in the open space in front of the Wirthshaus, where the lights from the windows illumined their faces. There I saw the broad-shouldered Lydia, Rosine, Doroty, and all the rest, in their Sunday clothes, flushed, laughing, and chattering; but no Wilhelmina.

'Where can she be?' I said.

If she was there, the larger girls concealed her with their buxom breadth; I looked for the slender little maiden in vain.

'Shu!' cried the girls, 'de bugle!'

Far down the station road we heard the bugle and saw the glimmering of lights among the trees. On it came, a will-o' the-wisp procession, first a detachment of village boys each with a lantern or torch, next the returned soldiers winding their bugles,—for, German-like, they all had musical instruments,—then an excited crowd of brothers and cousins loaded with knapsacks, guns, and military accoutrements of all kinds; each man had something, were it only a tin cup, and proudly they marched in the footsteps of their glorious relatives, bearing the spoils of war. The girls set up a shrill cry of welcome as the procession approached, but the ranks continued unbroken until the open space in front of the Wirthshaus was reached; then, at a signal, the soldiers gave three cheers, the villagers joining in with all their hearts and lungs, but wildly and out of time, like the scattering fire of an awkward squad. The sound had never been heard in Zoar before. The soldiers gave a final 'Tiger-r-r!' and then broke ranks, mingling with the excited crowd, exchanging greetings and embraces. All talked at once; some wept, some laughed; and through it all silently stood the three trustees on the dark porch in front of the store, looking down upon their wild flock, their sober faces visible in the glare of the torches and lanterns below. The entire population was present; even the babies were held up on the outskirts of the crowd, stolid and staring.

'Where can Wilhelmina be?' I said again.

'Here, under the window; I saw her long ago,' replied one of the women.

Leaning against a piazza-pillar, close under my eyes, stood the little maiden, pale and still. I could not disguise from myself that she looked almost ugly among those florid, laughing girls, for her color was gone, and her eyes so fixed that they looked unnaturally large; her somewhat heavy Egyptian features stood out in the bright light, but her small form was lost among the group of broad, white-kerchiefed shoulders, adorned with breast-knots of gay flowers. And had Wilhelmina no flower? She, so fond of blossoms? I looked again; yes, a little white rose, drooping and pale as herself.

But where was Gustav? The soldiers came and went in the crowd, and all spoke to Mina; but where was the One? I caught the landlord's little son as he passed, and asked the question.

'Gustav! Dat's him,' he answered, pointing out a tall, rollicking soldier who seemed to be embracing the whole population in his gleeful welcome. That very soldier had passed Mina a dozen times, flinging a gay greeting to her each time; but nothing more.

After half an hour of general rejoicing, the crowd dispersed, each household bearing off in triumph the hero that fell to its lot. Then the tiled domiciles, where usually all were asleep an hour after twilight, blazed forth with unaccustomed light from every little window; within we could see the circles, with flagons of beer and various dainties manufactured in secret during the day, sitting and talking together in a manner which, for Zoar, was a wild revel, since it was nearly eleven o'clock! We were not the only outside spectators of this unwonted gayety; several times we met the trustees stealing along in the shadow from house to house, like anxious spectres in broad-brimmed hats. No doubt they said to each other, 'How, how will this end!'

The merry Gustav had gone off by Mina's side, which gave me some comfort; but when in our rounds we came to the gardener's house and gazed through the open door, the little maiden sat apart, and the soldier, in the centre of an admiring circle, was telling stories of the war.

I felt a foreboding of sorrow as I gazed out through the little window before climbing up into my high bed. Lights still twinkled in some of the houses, but a white mist was rising from the river, and the drowsy long-drawn chant of the summer night invited me to dreamless sleep.

The next morning I could not resist questioning Jacobina, who also had her lover among the soldiers, if all was well.

'O yes. They stay,—all but two. We's married next mont.'

'And the two?'

'Karl and Gustav.'

'And Wilhelmina!' I exclaimed.

'O she let him go,' answered Jacobina, bringing fresh coffee.

'Poor child! How does she bear it?'

'O so. She cannot help. She say noding.'

'But the trustees, will they allow these young men to leave the Community?'

'They cannot help,' said Jacobina. 'Gustav and Karl write not in the book; they free to go. Wilhelmina marry Jacob; it's joost the same; all r-r-ight,' added Jacobina, who prided herself upon her English, caught from visitors at the Wirthshaus table.

'Ah! but it is not just the same,' I thought as I walked up to the garden to find my little maiden. She was not there; the leathery mother said she was out on the hills with the cows.

'So Gustav is going to leave the Community,' I said in German.

'Yes, better so. He is an idle, wild boy. Now Veelhelmeeny can marry the baker, a good steady man.'

'But Mina does not like him,' I suggested.

'Das macht nichts,' answered the leathery mother.

Wilhelmina was not in the pasture; I sought for her everywhere, and called her name. The poor child had hidden herself, and whether she heard me or not she did not respond. All day she kept herself aloof; I almost feared she would never return; but in the late twilight a little figure slipped through the garden-gate and took refuge in the house before I could speak; for I was watching for the child, apparently the only one, though a stranger, to care for her sorrow.

'Can I not see her?' I said to the leathery mother, following to the door.

'Eh, no; she's foolish; she will not speak a word; she has gone off to bed,' was the answer.

For three days I did not see Mina, so early did she flee away to the hills and so late return. I followed her to the pasture once or twice, but she would not show herself, and I could not discover her hiding place. The fourth day I learned that Gustav and Karl were to leave the village in the afternoon, probably forever. The other soldiers had signed the articles presented by the anxious trustees, and settled down into the old routine, going afield with the rest, although still heroes of the hour; they were all to be married in August. No doubt the hardships of their campaigns among the Tennessee mountains had taught them that the rich valley was a home not to be despised; nevertheless, it was evident that the flowers of the flock were those who were about departing, and that in Gustav and Karl the Community lost its brightest spirits. Evident to us; but possibly, the Community cared not for bright spirits.

I had made several attempts to speak to Gustav; this morning I at last succeeded. I found him polishing his bugle on the garden bench.

'Why are you going away, Gustav?' I asked. 'Zoar is a pleasant little village.'

'Too slow for me, miss.'

'The life is easy, however; you will find the world a hard place.'

'I don't mind work, ma'am, but I do like to be free. I feel all cramped up here, with these rules and bells; and, besides, I couldn't stand those trustees; they never let a fellow alone.'

'And Wilhelmina? If you do go, I hope you will take her with you or come for her when you have found work.'

'Oh no, miss. All that was long ago. It's all over now.'

'But you like her, Gustav.'

'O so. She's a good little thing, but too quiet for me.'

'But she likes you,' I said desperately, for I saw no other way to loosen this Gordian knot.

'O no, miss. She got used to it, and has thought of it all these years; that's all. She'll forget about it and marry the baker.'

'But she does not like the baker.'

'Why not? He's a good fellow enough. She'll like him in time. It's all the same. I declare it's too bad to see all these girls going on in the same old way, in their ugly gowns and big shoes! Why, ma'am, I could'nt, take Mina outside, even if I wanted to; she's too old to learn new ways, and everybody would laugh at her. She could'nt get along a day. Besides,' said the young soldier, coloring up to his eyes, 'I don't mind telling you that—that there's some one else. Look here, ma'am.'

And he put into my hand a card photograph representing a pretty girl, over dressed, and adorned with curls and gilt jewelery. 'That's Miss Martin,' said Gustav with pride; 'Miss Emmeline Martin, of Cincinnati. I'm going to marry Miss Martin.'

As I held the pretty, flashy picture in my hand, all my castles fell to the ground. My plan for taking Mina home with me, accustoming her gradually to other clothes and ways, teaching her enough of the world to enable her to hold her place without pain, my hope that my husband might find a situation for Gustav in some of the iron-mills near Cleveland, in short, all the idyl I had woven, was destroyed. If it had not been for this red-cheeked Miss Martin in her gilt beads! 'Why is it that men will be such fools?' I thought. Up sprung a memory of the curls and ponderous jet necklace I sported at a certain period of my existence, when John—I was silenced, gave Gustav his picture, and walked away without a word.

At noon the villagers, on their way back to work, paused at the Wirthshaus to say good bye; Karl and Gustav were there, and the old woolly horse had already gone to the station with their boxes. Among the others came Christine, Karl's former affianced, heartwhole and smiling, already betrothed to a new lover; but no Wilhelmina. Good wishes and farewells were exchanged, and at last the two soldiers started away, falling into the marching step and watched with furtive satisfaction by the three trustees, who stood together in the shadow of the smithy apparently deeply absorbed in a broken-down cask.

It was a lovely afternoon, and I, too, strolled down the station road embowered in shade. The two soldiers were not far in advance. I had passed the flour-mill on the outskirts of the village and was approaching the old quarry, when a sound startled me; out of the rocks in front rushed a little figure and crying 'Gustav, mein Gustav!' fell at the soldier's feet. It was Wilhelmina.

I ran forward and took her from the young men; she lay in my arms as if dead. The poor child was sadly changed; always slender and swaying, she now looked thin and shrunken, her skin had a strange, dark pallor, and her lips were drawn in as if from pain. I could see her eyes through the large-orbed thin lids, and the brown shadows beneath extended down into the cheeks.

'Was ist's?' said Gustav, looking bewildered. 'Is she sick?'

I answered 'Yes,' but nothing more. I could see that he had no suspicion of the truth, believing as he did that the 'good fellow' of a baker would do very well for this 'good little thing' who was 'too quiet' for him. The memory of Miss Martin sealed my lips. But if it had not been for that pretty, flashy picture, would I not have spoken!

'You must go; you will miss the train,' I said after a few minutes. 'I will see to Mina.'

But Gustav lingered. Perhaps he was really troubled to see the little sweetheart of his boyhood in such desolate plight; perhaps a touch of the old feeling came back; and perhaps also it was nothing of the kind, and, as usual, my romantic thoughts were carrying me away. At any rate, whatever it was, he stooped over the fainting girl.

'She looks bad,' he said, 'very bad. I wish— But she'll get well and marry the baker. Good bye, Mina.' And bending his tall form, he kissed her colorless cheek, and then hastened away to join the impatient Karl; a curve in the road soon hid them from view.

Wilhelmina had stirred at his touch; after a moment her large eyes opened slowly; she looked around as if dazed, but all at once memory came back and she started up with the same cry, 'Gustav, mein Gustav!' I drew her head down on my shoulder to stifle the sound; it was better the soldier should not hear it, and its anguish thrilled my own heart also. She had not the strength to resist me, and in a few minutes I knew that the young men were out of hearing as they strode on towards the station and out into the wide world.

The forest was solitary, we were beyond the village; all the afternoon I sat under the trees with the stricken girl. Again, as in her joy her words were few; again as in her joy her whole being was involved. Her little rough hands were cold, a film had gathered over her eyes; she did not weep, but moaned to herself, and all her senses seemed blunted. At nightfall I took her home, and the leathery mother received her with a frown; but the child was beyond caring, and crept away, dumbly, to her room.

The next morning she was off to the hills again, nor could I find her for several days. Evidently in spite of my sympathy I was no more to her than I should have been to a wounded fawn. She was a mixture of the wild, shy creature of the woods and the deep-loving woman of the tropics; in either case I could be but small comfort. When at last I did see her, she was apathetic and dull; her feelings, her senses, and her intelligence seemed to have gone within, as if preying upon her heart. She scarcely listened to my proposal to take her with me; for in my pity I had suggested it, in spite of its difficulties.

'No,' she said, mechanically, 'I'se better here'; and fell into silence again.

A month later a friend went down to spend a few days in the valley, and upon her return described to us the weddings of the whilom soldiers. 'It was really a pretty sight,' she said, 'the quaint peasant dresses and the flowers. Afterwards, the band went round the village playing their odd tunes, and all had a holiday. There were two civilians married also; I mean two young men who had not been to the war. It seems that two of the soldiers turned their backs upon the Community and their allotted brides, and marched away; but the Zoar maidens are not romantic, I fancy, for these two deserted ones were betrothed again, and married, all in the short space of four weeks.'

'Was not one Wilhelmina, the gardener's daughter, a short, dark girl?' I asked.

'Yes.'

'And she married Jacob the baker?'

'Yes.'

The next year, weary of the cold lake-winds, we left the icy shore and went down to the valley to meet the coming spring, finding her already there, decked with vines and flowers. A new waitress brought us our coffee.

'How is Wilhelmina?' I asked.

'Eh,—Wilhelmina? O, she not here now; she gone to the Next Country,' answered the girl in a matter-of-fact way. 'She die last October, and Jacob he have anoder wife now.'

In the late afternoon I asked a little girl to show me Wilhelmina's grave in the quiet God's Acre on the hill. Innovation was creeping in, even here; the later graves had mounds raised over them, and one had a little head-board with an inscription in ink.

Wilhelmina lay apart, and some one, probably the old gardener, who had loved her in his silent way, had planted a rose-bush at the head of the mound. I dismissed my guide and sat there in the sunset, thinking of many things, but chiefly of this: 'Why should this great wealth of love have been allowed to waste itself? Why is it that the greatest of power, unquestionably, of this mortal life should so often seem a useless gift?'

No answer came from the sunset clouds, and as twilight sank down on the earth I rose to go. 'I fully believe,' I said, as though repeating a creed, 'that this poor, loving heart, whose earthly body lies under this mound, is happy in its own loving way. It has not been changed, but the happiness it longed for has come. How we know not; but the God who made Wilhelmina understands her. He has given unto her not rest, not peace, but an active, living joy.'

I walked away through the wild meadow, under whose turf, unmarked by stone or mound, lay the first pioneers of the Community and out into the forest road, untravelled save when the dead passed over it to their last earthly home. The evening was still and breathless, and the shadows lay thick on the grass as I looked back. But I could still distinguish the little mound with the rose-bush at its head, and, not without tears, I said, 'Farewell, poor Wilhelmina; farewell.'

ST. CLAIR FLATS

IN September, 1855, I first saw the St. Clair Flats. Owing to Raymond's determination, we stopped there.

'Why go on?' he asked. 'Why cross another long, rough lake, when here is all we want?'

'But no one ever stops here,' I said.

'So much the better; we shall have it all to ourselves.'

'But we must at least have a roof over our heads.'

'I presume we can find one.'

The captain of the steamer, however, knew of no roof save that covering a little lighthouse set on spiles, which the boat would pass within the half hour; we decided to get off there, and throw ourselves upon the charity of the lighthouse-man. In the meantime, we sat on the bow with Captain Kidd, our four-legged companion, who had often accompanied us on hunt-expeditions, but never so far westward. It had been rough on Lake Erie,—very rough. We, who had sailed the ocean with composure, found ourselves most inhumanly tossed on the short chopping waves of this fresh water sea; we, who alone of all the cabin-list had eaten our four courses every day on the ocean-steamer, found ourselves here reduced to the depressing diet of a herring and pilot-bread. Captain Kidd, too, had suffered dumbly; even now he could not find comfort, but tried every plank in the deck, one after the other, circling round and round after his tail dog-fashion, before lying down, and no sooner down than up again, for another choice of planks, another circling, and another failure. We were sailing across a small lake whose smooth waters were like clear green oil; as we drew near the outlet, the low, green shores curved inward and came together, and the steamer entered a narrow, green river.

'Here we are,' said Raymond. 'Now we can soon land.'

'But there isn't any land,' I answered.

'What is that, then?' asked my near-sighted companion, pointing toward what seemed a shore.

'Reeds.'

'And what do they run back to?'

'Nothing.'

'But there must be solid ground beyond?'

'Nothing but reeds, flags, lily-pads, grass, and water, as far as I can see.'

'A marsh?'

'Yes, a marsh.'

The word 'marsh' does not bring up a beautiful picture to the mind, and yet the reality was as beautiful as anything I have ever seen,—an enchanted land, whose memory haunts me as an idea unwritten, a melody unsung, a picture unpainted, haunts the artist, and will not away. On each side and in front, as far as the eye could reach, stretched the low green land which was yet no land, intersected by hundreds of channels, narrow and broad, whose waters were green as their shores. In and out, now running into each other for a moment, now setting off each for himself again, these many channels flowed along with a rippling current; zigzag as they were, they never seemed to loiter, but, as if knowing just where they were going and what they had to do, they found time to take their own pleasant roundabout way, visiting the secluded households of their friends the flags, who, poor souls, must always stay at home. These currents were as clear as crystal, and green as the water-grasses that fringed their miniature shores. The bristling reeds, like companies of free-lances, rode boldly out here and there into the deeps, trying to conquer more territory for the grasses, but the currents were hard to conquer; they dismounted the free-lances, and flowed over their submerged heads; they beat them down with assaulting ripples; they broke their backs so effectually that the bravest had no spirit left, but trailed along, limp and bedraggled. And, if by chance the lances succeeded in stretching their forces across from one little shore to another, then the unconquered currents forced their way between the closely serried ranks of the enemy, and flowed on as gayly as ever, leaving the grasses sitting hopeless on the bank; for they needed solid ground for their delicate feet, these graceful ladies in green.

You might call it a marsh; but there was no mud, no dark slimy water, no stagnant scum; there were no rank yellow lilies, no gormandizing frogs, no swinish mud-turtles. The clear waters of the channels ran over golden sands, and hurtled among the stiff reeds so swiftly that only in a bay, or where protected by a crescent point, could the fair white lilies float in the quiet their serene beauty requires. The flags, who brandished their swords proudly, were martinets down to their very heels, keeping themselves as clean under the water as above, and harboring not a speck of mud on their bright green uniforms. For inhabitants, there were small fish roving about here and there in the clear tide, keeping an eye out for the herons, who, watery as to legs, but venerable and wise of aspect, stood on promontories musing, apparently, on the secrets of the ages.

The steamer's route was a constant curve; through the larger channels of the archipelago she wound, as if following the clew of a labyrinth. By turns she headed toward all the points of the compass, finding a channel where, to our uninitiated eyes, there was no channel, doubling upon her own track, going broadside foremost, floundering and backing, like a whale caught in a shallow. Here, landlocked, she would choose what seemed the narrowest channel of all, and dash recklessly through, with the reeds almost brushing her sides; there she crept gingerly along a broad expanse of water, her paddle-wheels scarcely revolving, in the excess of her caution. Saplings, with their heads of foliage on, and branches adorned with fluttering rags, served as finger-posts to show the way through the watery defiles, and there were many other hieroglyphics legible only to the pilot. 'This time, surely, we shall run ashore,' we thought again and again, as the steamer glided, head-on, toward an islet; but at the last there was always a quick turn into some unseen strait opening like a secret passage in a castle-wall, and we found ourselves in a new lakelet, heading in the opposite direction. Once we met another steamer, and the two great hulls floated slowly past each other, with engines motionless, so near that the passengers could have shaken hands with each other had they been so disposed. Not that they were so disposed, however; far from it. They gathered on their respective decks and gazed at each other gravely; not a smile was seen, not a word spoken, not the shadow of a salutation given. It was not pride, it was not suspicion; it was the universal listlessness of the travelling American bereft of his business, Othello with his occupation gone. What can such a man do on a steamer? Generally, nothing. Certainly he would never think of any such light-hearted nonsense as a smile or passing bow.

But the ships were, *par excellence*, the bewitched craft, the Flying Dutchmen of the Flats. A brig, with lofty, sky-scraping sails, bound south, came into view of our steamer, bound north, and passed, we hugging the shore to give her room: five minutes afterward the sky-scraping sails we had left behind veered around in front of us again; another five minutes, and there they were far distant on the right; another, and there they were again close by us on the left. For half an hour those sails circled around us, and yet all the time we were pushing steadily forward; this seemed witching work indeed. Again, the numerous schooners thought nothing of sailing over-land; we saw them on all sides gliding before the wind, or beating up against it over the windows as easily as over the water; sailing on grass was a mere trifle to these spirit-barks. All this we saw, as I said before, apparently. But in that adverb is hidden the magic of the St. Clair Flats.

'It is beautiful,—beautiful,' I said, looking off over the vivid green expanse.

'Beautiful?' echoed the captain, who had himself taken charge of the steering when the steamer entered the labyrinth,—'I don't see anything beautiful in it!—Port your helm up there; port!'

'Port it is, sir,' came back from the pilot-house above.

'These Flats give us more trouble than any other spot on the lakes; vessels are all the time getting aground and blocking up the way, which is narrow enough at best. There's some talk of Uncle Sam's cutting a canal right through,—a straight canal; but he's so slow, Uncle Sam is, and I'm afraid I'll be off the waters before the job is done.'

'A straight canal!' I repeated, thinking with dismay of an ugly utilitarian ditch invading this beautiful winding waste of green.

'Yes, you can see for yourself what a saving it would be,' replied the captain. 'We could run right through in no time, day or night; whereas, now, we have to turn and twist and watch every inch of the whole everlasting marsh.' Such was the captain's opinion. But we, albeit neither romantic nor artistic, were captivated with his 'everlasting marsh,' and eager to penetrate far within its green fastnesses.

'I suppose there are other families living about here, besides the family at the lighthouse?' I said.

'Never heard of any; they'd have to live on a raft if they did.'

'But there must be some solid ground.'

'Don't believe it; it's nothing but one great sponge for miles.—Steady up there; steady!'

'Very well,' said Raymond, 'so be it. If there is only the lighthouse, at the lighthouse we'll get off, and take our chances.'

'You're surveyors, I suppose?' said the captain.

Surveyors are the pioneers of the lake-country, understood by the people to be a set of harmless monomaniacs, given to building little observatories along-shore, where there is nothing to observe; mild madmen, whose vagaries and instruments are equally singular. As surveyors, therefore, the captain saw nothing surprising in our determination to get off at the lighthouse; if we had proposed going ashore on a plank in the middle of Lake Huron, he would have made no objection.

At length the lighthouse came into view, a little fortress perched on spiles, with a ladder for entrance; as usual in small houses, much time seemed devoted to washing, for a large crane, swung to and fro by a rope, extended out over the water, covered with fluttering garments hung out to dry. The steamer lay to, our row-boat was launched, our traps handed out, Captain Kidd took his place in the bow, and we pushed off into the shallows; then the great paddle-wheels revolved again, and the steamer sailed away, leaving us astern, rocking on her waves, and watched listlessly by the passengers until a turn hid us from their view. In the mean time numerous flaxen-haired children had appeared at the little windows of the lighthouse,—too many of them, indeed, for our hopes of comfort.

'Ten,' said Raymond, counting heads.

The ten, moved by curiosity as we approached, hung out of the windows so far that they held on merely by their ankles.

'We cannot possibly save them all,' I remarked, looking up at the dangling gazers.

'O, they're amphibious,' said Raymond; 'web-footed, I presume.'

We rowed up under the fortress, and demanded parley with the keeper in the following language:—

'Is your father here?'

'No; but ma is,' answered the chorus.—'Ma! ma!'

Ma appeared, a portly female, who held converse with us from the top of the ladder. The sum and substance of the dialogue was that she had not a corner to give us, and recommended us to find Liakim, and have him show us the way to Waiting Samuel's.

'Waiting Samuel's?' we repeated.

'Yes; he's a kind of crazy man living away over there in the Flats. But there's no harm in him, and his wife is a tidy housekeeper. You be surveyors, I suppose?'

We accepted the imputation in order to avoid a broadside of questions, and asked the whereabouts of Liakim.

'O, he's round the point, somewhere there, fishing!'

We rowed on and found him, a little, round-shouldered man, in an old flat-bottomed boat, who had not taken a fish, and looked as though he never would. We explained our errand.

'Did Rosabel Lee tell ye to come to me?' he asked.

'The woman in the lighthouse told us,' I said.

'That's Rosabel Lee, that's my wife; I'm Liakim Lee,' said the little man, gathering together his forlorn old rods and tackle, and pulling up his anchor.

"In the kingdom down by the sea
Lived the beautiful Annabel Lee,"

I quoted, *sotto voce.*

'And what very remarkable feet had she!' added Raymond, improvising under the inspiration of certain shoes, scow-like in shape, gigantic in length and breadth, which had made themselves visible at the top round of the ladder.

At length the shabby old boat got under way, and we followed in its path, turning off to the right through a network of channels, now pulling ourselves along by the reeds, now paddling over a raft of lily-pads, now poling through a winding labyrinth, and now rowing with broad sweeps across the little lake. The sun was sinking, and the western sky grew bright at his coming; there was not a cloud to make mountain-peaks on the horizon, nothing but the level earth below meeting the curved sky above, so evenly and clearly that it seemed as though we could go out there and touch it with our hands. Soon we lost sight of the little lighthouse; then one by one the distant sails sank down and disappeared, and we were left alone on the grassy sea, rowing toward the sunset.

'We must have come a mile or two, and there is no sign of a house,' I called out to our guide.

'Well, I don't pretend to know how far it is, exactly,' replied Liakim; 'we don't know how far anything is here in the Flats, we don't.'

'But are you sure you know the way?'

'O my, yes! We've got most to the boy. There it is!'

The 'boy' was a buoy, a fragment of plank painted white, part of the cabin-work of some wrecked steamer.

'Now, then,' said Liakim, pausing, 'you jest go straight on in this here channel till you come to the ninth run from this boy, on the right; take that, and it will lead you right up to Waiting Samuel's door.'

'Aren't you coming with us?'

'Well, no. In the first place, Rosabel Lee will be waiting supper for me, and she don't like to wait; and, besides, Samuel can't abide to see none of us round his part of the Flats.'

'But—' I began.

'Let him go,' interposed Raymond; 'we can find the house without trouble.' And he tossed a silver dollar to the little man, who was already turning his boat.

'Thank you,' said Liakim. 'Be sure you take the ninth run and no other,—the ninth run from this boy. If you make any mistake, you'll find yourselves miles away.'

With this cheerful statement, he began to row back. I did not altogether fancy being left on the watery waste without a guide; the name, too, of our mythic host did not bring up a certainty of supper and beds. 'Waiting Samuel,' I repeated, doubtfully. 'What is he waiting for?' I called back over my shoulder; for Raymond was rowing.

'The judgment-day!' answered Liakim, in a shrill key. The boats were now far apart; another turn, and we were alone.

We glided on, counting the runs on the right: some were wide, promising rivers; others wee little rivulets; the eighth was far away; and, when we had passed it, we could hardly decide whether we had reached the ninth or not, so small was the opening, so choked with weeds, showing scarcely a gleam of water beyond when we stood up to inspect it.

'It is certainly the ninth, and I vote that we try it. It will do as well as another, and I for one, am in no hurry to arrive anywhere,' said Raymond, pushing the boat in among the reeds.

'Do you want to lose yourself in this wilderness?' I asked, making a flag of my handkerchief to mark the spot where we had left the main stream.

'I think we are lost already,' was the calm reply. I began to fear we were.

For some distance the 'run,' as Liakim called it, continued choked with aquatic vegetation, which acted like so many devil-fish catching our oars; at length it widened and gradually gave us a clear channel, albeit so winding and erratic that the glow of the sunset, our only beacon, seemed to be executing a waltz all round the horizon. At length we saw a dark spot on the left, and distinguished the outline of a low house. 'There it is,' I said, plying my oars with renewed strength. But the run turned short off in the opposite direction, and the house disappeared. After some time it rose again, this time on our right, but once more the run turned its back and shot off on a tangent. The sun had gone, and the rapid twilight of September was falling around us; the air, however, was singularly clear, and, as there was absolutely nothing to make a shadow, the darkness came on evenly over the level green. I was growing anxious, when a third time the house appeared, but the wilful run passed by it, although so near that we could distinguish its open windows and door, 'Why not get out and wade across?' I suggested.

'According to Liakim, it is the duty of this run to take us to the very door of Waiting Samuel's mansion, and it shall take us,' said Raymond, rowing on. It did.

Doubling upon itself in the most unexpected manner, it brought us back to a little island, where the tall grass had given way to a vegetable-garden. We landed, secured our boat, and walked up the pathway toward the house. In the dusk it seemed to be a low, square structure, built of planks covered with plaster; the roof was flat, the windows unusually broad, the door stood open,—but no one appeared. We knocked. A voice from within called out, 'Who are you, and what do you want with Waiting Samuel?'

'Pilgrims, asking for food and shelter,' replied Raymond.

'Do you know the ways of righteousness?'

'We can learn them.'

'We can learn them,' I echoed.

'Will you conform to the rules of this household without murmuring?'

'We will.'

'Enter then and peace be with you!' said the voice drawing nearer. We stepped cautiously through the dark passage into a room, whose open windows let in sufficient twilight to show us a shadowy figure. 'Seat yourselves,' it said. We found a bench, and sat down.

'What seek ye here?' continued the shadow.

'Rest!' replied Raymond.

'Hunting and fishing!' I added.

'Ye will find more than rest,' said the voice, ignoring me altogether (I am often ignored in this way),—'more than rest, if ye stay long enough, and learn of the hidden treasures. Are you willing to seek for them?'

'Certainly!' said Raymond. 'Where shall we dig?'

'I speak not of earthly digging, young man. Will you give me the charge of your souls?'

'Certainly, if you will also take charge of our bodies.'

'Supper, for instance,' I said, again coming to the front; 'and beds.'

The shadow groaned; then it called out wearily, 'Roxana!'

'Yes, Samuel,' replied an answering voice, and a second shadow became dimly visible on the threshold. 'The woman will attend to your earthly concerns,' said Waiting Samuel.—'Roxana, take them hence.' The second shadow came forward, and, without a word, took our hands and led us along the dark passage like two children, warning us now of a step, now of a turn, then of two steps, and finally opening a door and ushering us into a fire-lighted room. Peat was burning upon the wide hearth, and a singing kettle hung above it on a crane; the red glow shone on a rough table, chairs cushioned in bright calico, a loud ticking clock, a few gayly flowered plates and cups on a shelf, shining tins against the plastered wall, and a cat dozing on a bit of carpet in one corner. The cheery domestic scene, coming after the wide, dusky Flats, the silence, the darkness, and the mystical words of the shadowy Samuel, seemed so real and pleasant that my heart grew light within me.

'What a bright fire!' I said. 'This is your domain, I suppose, Mrs.—Mrs.—'

'I am not Mrs.; I am called Roxana,' replied the woman, busying herself at the hearth.

'Ah, you are then the sister of Waiting Samuel, I presume?'

'No, I am his wife, fast enough; we were married by the minister twenty years ago. But that was before Samuel had seen any visions.'

'Does he see visions?'

'Yes, almost every day.'

'Do you see them, also?'

'O no; I'm not like Samuel. He has great gifts, Samuel has! The visions told us to come here; we used to live away down in Maine.'

'Indeed! That was a long journey!'

'Yes! And we didn't come straight either. We'd get to one place and stop, and I'd think we were going to stay, and just get things comfortable, when Samuel would see another vision, and we'd have to start on. We wandered in that way two or three years, but at last we got here, and something in the Flats seemed to suit the spirits, and they let us stay.'

At this moment, through the half-open door, came a voice.

'An evil beast is in this house. Let him depart.'

'Do you mean me?' said Raymond, who had made himself comfortable in a rocking-chair.

'Nay; I refer to the four-legged beast,' continued the voice. 'Come forth, Apollyon!'

Poor Captain Kidd seemed to feel that he was the person in question, for he hastened under the table with drooping tail and mortified aspect.

'Roxana, send forth the beast,' said the voice.

The woman put down her dishes and went toward the table; but I interposed.

'If he must go, I will take him,' I said, rising.

'Yes; he must go,' replied Roxana, holding open the door. So I ordered out the unwilling Captain, and led him into the passageway.

'Out of the house, out of the house,' said Waiting Samuel. 'His feet may not rest upon this sacred ground. I must take him hence in the boat.'

'But where?'

'Across the channel there is an islet large enough for him; he shall have food and shelter, but here he cannot abide,' said the man, leading the way down to the boat.

The Captain was therefore ferried across, a tent was made for him out of some old mats, food was provided, and, lest he should swim back, he was tethered by a long rope, which allowed him to prowl around his domain and take his choice of three runs for drinking-water. With all these advantages, the ungrateful animal persisted in howling dismally as we rowed away. It was company he wanted, and not a 'dear little isle of his own'; but then, he was not by nature poetical.

'You do not like dogs?' I said, as we reached our strand again.

'St. Paul wrote, 'Beware of dogs,' replied Samuel.

'But did he mean—'

'I argue not with unbelievers; his meaning is clear to me, let that suffice,' said my strange host, turning away and leaving me to find my way back alone. A delicious repast was awaiting me. Years have gone by, the world and all its delicacies have been unrolled before me, but the memory of the meals I ate in that little kitchen in the Flats haunts me still. That night it was only fish, potatoes, biscuit, butter, stewed fruit, and coffee; but the fish was fresh, and done to the turn of a perfect broil, not burn; the potatoes were fried to a rare crisp, yet tender perfection, not chippy brittleness; the biscuits were light, flaked creamily, and brown on the bottom; the butter freshly churned, without salt; the fruit, great pears, with their cores extracted, standing whole on their dish, ready to melt, but not melted; and the coffee clear and strong, with yellow cream and the old-fashioned, unadulterated loaf-sugar. We ate. That does not express it; we devoured. Roxana waited on us, and warmed up into something like excitement under our praises.

'I *do* like good cooking,' she confessed. 'It's about all I have left of my old life. I go over to the mainland for supplies, and in the winter I try all kinds of new things to pass away the time. But Samuel is a poor eater, he is; and so there isn't much comfort in it. I'm mighty glad you've come, and I hope you'll stay as long as you find it pleasant.' This we promised to do, as we finished the potatoes and attacked the great jellied pears. 'There's one thing, though,' continued Roxana; 'you'll have to come to our service on the roof at sunrise.'

'What service?' I asked.

'The invocation. Dawn is a holy time, Samuel says, and we always wait for it; 'before the morning watch,' you know,—it says so in the Bible. Why, my name means 'the dawn,' Samuel says; that's the reason he gave it to me. My real name, down in Maine, was Maria,—Maria Ann.'

'But I may not wake in time,' I said.

'Samuel will call you.'

'And if, in spite of that, I should sleep over?'

'You would not do that; it would vex him,' replied Roxana calmly.

'Do you believe in these visions, madam?' asked Raymond, as we left the table, and seated ourselves in front of the dying fire.

'Yes,' said Roxana; emphasis was unnecessary, of course she believed.

'Almost every day there is a spiritual presence, but it does not always speak. They come and hold long conversations in the winter, when there is nothing else to do; that I think is very kind of them, for in the summer Samuel can fish and his time is more occupied. There were fisherman in the Bible, you know; it is a holy calling.'

'Does Samuel ever go over to the mainland?'

'No, he never leaves the Flats. I do all the business; take over the fish, and buy the supplies. I bought all our cattle,' said Roxana, with pride. 'I poled them away over here on a raft, one by one, when they were little things.'

'Where do you pasture them?'

'Here on the island; there are only a few acres, to be sure; but I can cut boat-loads of the best feed within a stone's throw. If we only had a little more solid ground! But this island is almost the only solid piece in the Flats.'

'Your butter is certainly delicious.'

'Yes, I do my best. It is sold to the steamers and vessels as fast as I make it.'

'You keep yourself busy, I see.'

'O, I like to work; I could'nt get on without it.'

'And Samuel?'

'He is not like me,' replied Roxana. 'He has great gifts, Samuel has. I often think how strange it is that I should be the wife of such a holy man! He is very kind to me, too; he tells me about the visions, and all the other things.'

'What things?' said Raymond.

'The spirits, and the sacred influence of the sun; the fiery triangle, and the thousand years of joy. The great day is coming, you know; Samuel is waiting for it.'

'Nine of the night. Take thou thy rest. I will lay me down in peace, and sleep, for it is thou, Lord, only, that makest me dwell in safety,' chanted a voice in the hall; the tone was deep and not without melody, and the words singularly impressive in that still, remote place.

'Go,' said Roxana, instantly pushing aside her half-washed dishes. 'Samuel will take you to your room.'

'Do you leave your work unfinished?' I said, with some curiosity, noticing that she had folded her hands without even hanging up her towels.

'We do nothing after the evening chant,' she said. 'Pray go; he is waiting.'

'Can we have candles?'

'Waiting Samuel allows no false lights in his house; as imitations of the glorious sun, they are abominable to him. Go, I beg.'

She opened the door, and we went into the passage; it was entirely dark, but the man led us across to our room, showed us the position of our beds by sense of feeling, and left us without a word. After he had gone, we struck matches, one by one, and, with the aid of their uncertain light, managed to get into our respective mounds in safety; they were shake-downs on the floor, made of fragrant hay instead of straw, covered with beautifully clean white sheets and patchwork coverlids, and provided with large, luxurious pillows. O pillow! Has any one sung thy praises? When tired or sick, when discouraged or sad, what gives so much comfort as a pillow? Not your curled hair brickbats; not your stiff, fluted, rasping covers, or limp cotton cases; but a good, generous, soft pillow, deftly cased in smooth, cool, untrimmed linen! There's a friend for you, a friend who changes not, a friend who soothes all your troubles with a soft caress, a mesmeric touch of balmy forgetfulness.

I slept a dreamless sleep. Then I heard a voice borne toward me as if coming from far over a sea, the waves bringing it nearer and nearer.

'Awake!' it cried; 'awake! The night is far spent; the day is at hand. Awake!'

I wondered vaguely over this voice as to what manner of voice it might be, but it came again, and again, and finally I awoke to find it at my side. The gray light of dawn came through the open windows, and Raymond was already up, engaged with a tub of water and crash towels. Again the chant sounded in my ears.

'Very well, very well,' I said, testily. 'But if you sing before breakfast you'll cry before night, Waiting Samuel.'

Our host had disappeared, however, without hearing my flippant speech, and slowly I rose from my fragrant couch; the room was empty save for our two mounds, two tubs of water, and a number of towels hanging on nails. 'Not overcrowded with furniture,' I remarked.

'From Maine to Florida, from Massachusetts to Missouri, have I travelled, and never before found water enough,' said Raymond. 'If waiting for the judgment day raises such liberal ideas of tubs and towels, I would that all the hotel-keepers in the land could be convened here to take a lesson.'

Our green hunting-clothes were soon donned, and we went out into the hall; a flight of broad steps led up to the roof; Roxana appeared at the top and beckoned us thither. We ascended, and found ourselves on the flat roof. Samuel stood with his face toward the east and his arms outstretched, watching the horizon; behind was Roxana, with her hands clasped on her breast and her head bowed: thus they waited. The eastern sky was bright with golden light; rays shot upward toward the zenith, where the rose-lights of dawn were retreating down to the west, which still lay in the shadow of night; there was not a sound; the Flats stretched out dusky and still. Two or three minutes passed, and then a dazzling rim appeared above the horizon, and the first gleam of sunshine was shed over the level earth; simultaneously the two began a chant, simple as a Gregorian, but rendered in correct full tones. The words, apparently, had been collected from the Bible:—

"The heavens declare the glory of God—
Joy cometh in the morning!
In them is laid out the path of the sun—
Joy cometh in the morning!
As a bride groom goeth he forth;
As a strong man runneth his race,
The outgoings of the morning
Praise thee, O Lord!
Like a pelican in the wilderness,
Like a sparrow upon the house top,
I wait for the Lord.
It is good that we hope and wait,
Wait—wait.

The chant over, the two stood a moment silently, as if in contemplation, and then descended, passing us without a word or sign, with their hands clasped before them as though forming part of an unseen procession. Raymond and I were left alone upon the house-top.

'After all, it is not such a bad opening for a day; and there is the pelican of the wilderness to emphasize it,' I said, as a heron flew up from the water, and, slowly flapping his great wings, sailed across to another channel. As the sun rose higher, the birds began to sing; first a single note here and there, then a little trilling solo, and finally an outpouring of melody on all sides,—land-birds and water-birds, birds that lived in the Flats, and birds that had flown thither for breakfast,—the whole waste was awake and rejoicing in the sunshine.

'What a wild place it is!' said Raymond. 'How boundless it looks! One hill in the distance, one dark line of forest, even one tree, would break its charm. I have seen the ocean, I have seen the prairies, I have seen the great desert, but this is like a mixture of the three. It is an ocean full of land,—a prairie full of water,—a desert full of verdure.'

'Whatever it is, we shall find in it fishing and aquatic hunting to our hearts' content,' I answered.

And we did. After a breakfast delicious as the supper, we took our boat and a lunch-basket, and set out. 'But how shall we ever find our way back?'

I said, pausing as I recalled the network of runs, and the will-o'-the-wisp aspect of the house, the previous evening.

'There is no other way but to take a large ball of cord with you, fasten one end on shore, and let it run out over the stern of the boat,' said Roxana. 'Let it run out loosely, and it will float on the water. When you want to come back you can turn around and wind it in as you come. *I* can read the Flats like a book, but they're very blinding to most people; and you might keep going round in a circle. You will do better not to go far, anyway. I'll wind the bugle on the roof an hour before sunset; you can start back when you hear it; for it's awkward getting supper after dark.' With this musical promise we took the clew of twine which Roxana rigged for us in the stern of our boat, and started away, first releasing Captain Kidd, who was pacing his islet in sullen majesty, like another Napoleon on St. Helena. We took a new channel and passed behind the house, where the imported cattle were feeding in their little pasture; but the winding stream soon bore us away, the house sank out of sight, and we were left alone.

We had fine sport that morning among the ducks,—wood, teal, and canvas-back,—shooting from behind our screens woven of rushes; later in the day we took to fishing. The sun shone down, but there was a cool September breeze, and the freshness of the verdure was like early spring. At noon we took our lunch and a *siesta* among the water-lilies. When we awoke we found that a bittern had taken up his position near by, and was surveying us gravely:—

"'The moping bittern, motionless and stiff,
That on a stone so silently and stilly
Stands, an apparent sentinel, as if
To guard the water-lily,'"

quoted Raymond. The solemn bird, in his dark uniform, seemed quite undisturbed by our presence; yellow-throats and swamp-sparrows also came in numbers to have a look at us; and the fish swam up to the surface and eyed us curiously. Lying at ease in the boat, we in our turn looked down into the water. There is a singular fascination in looking down into a clear stream as the boat floats above; the mosses and twining water-plants seem to have arbors and grottoes in their recesses, where delicate marine creatures might live, naiads and mermaids of miniature size; at least we are always looking for them. There is a fancy, too, that one may find something,—a ring dropped from fair fingers idly trailing in the water; a book which the fishes have read thoroughly; a scarf caught among the lilies; a spoon with unknown initials; a drenched ribbon, or an embroidered handkerchief. None of these things did we find, but we did discover an old brass breastpin, whose probable glass stone was gone. It was a paltry trinket at best, but I fished it out with superstitious care,—a treasure-trove of the Flats. '"Drowned,"' I said, pathetically, '"drowned in her white robes—"'

'And brass breastpin,' added Raymond, who objected to sentiment, true or false.

'You Philistine! Is nothing sacred to you?'

'Not brass jewelry, certainly.'

'Take some lilies and consider them,' I said, plucking several of the queenly blossoms floating along-side.

"Cleopatra art thou, regal blossom,
Floating in thy galley down the Nile,—
All my soul does homage to thy splendor,
All my heart grows warmer in thy smile;
Yet thou smilest for thine own grand pleasure,
Caring not for all the world beside,
As in insolence of perfect beauty,
Sailest thou in silence down the tide.

"Loving, humble river all pursue thee,
Wafted are their kisses at thy feet;
Fiery sun himself cannot subdue thee,
Calm thou smilest through his raging heat;
Naught to thee the earth's great crowd of blossoms,
Naught to thee the rose-queen on her throne;
Haughty empress of the summer waters,
Livest thou, and diest, all alone."

This from Raymond.

'Where did you find that?' I asked.

'It is my own.'

'Of course! I might have known it. There is a certain rawness of style and versification which—'

'That's right,' interrupted Raymond; 'I know just what you are going to say. The whole matter of opinion is a game of 'follow-my-leader'; not one of you dares admire anything unless the critics say so. If I had told you the verses were by somebody instead of a nobody, you would have found wonderful beauties in them.'

'Exactly. My motto is, 'Never read anything unless it is by a somebody.' For, don't you see, that a nobody, if he is worth anything, will grow into a somebody, and, if he isn't worth anything you will have saved your time!'

'But it is not merely a question of growing,' said Raymond; 'it is a question of critics.'

'No; there you are mistaken. All the critics in the world can neither make nor crush a true poet.'

'What is poetry?' said Raymond, gloomily.

At this comprehensive question, the bittern gave a hollow croak, and flew away with his long legs trailing behind him. Probably he was not of an æsthetic turn of mind, and dreaded lest I should give a ramified answer.

Through the afternoon we fished when the fancy struck us, but most of the time we floated idly, enjoying the wild freedom of the watery waste. We watched the infinite varieties of the grasses, feathery, lance-leaved, tufted, drooping, banner-like, the deer's tongue, the wild-celery, and the so-called wild-rice, besides many unknown beauties delicately fringed, as difficult to catch and hold as thistle-down. There were plants journeying to and fro on the water like nomadic tribes of the desert; there were fleets of green leaves floating down the current; and now and then we saw a wonderful flower with scarlet bells but could never approach near enough to touch it.

At length, the distant sound of the bugle came to us on the breeze, and I slowly wound in the clew, directing Raymond as he pushed the boat along, backing water with the oars. The sound seemed to come from every direction. There was nothing for it to echo against, but, in place of the echo, we heard a long, dying cadence, which sounded on over the Flats fainter and fainter in a sweet, slender note, until a new tone broke forth. The music floated around us, now on one side, now on the other; if it had been our only guide, we should have been completely bewildered. But I wound the cord steadily; and at last suddenly, there before us, appeared the house with Roxana on the roof, her figure outlined against the sky. Seeing us, she played a final salute, and then descended, carrying the imprisoned music with her.

That night we had our supper at sunset. Waiting Samuel had his meals by himself in the front room. 'So that in case the spirits come, I shall not be there to hinder them,' explained Roxana. 'I am not holy, like Samuel; they will not speak before me.'

'Do you have your meals apart in the winter, also?' asked Raymond.

'Yes.'

'That is not very sociable,' I said.

'Samuel never was sociable,' replied Roxana. 'Only common folks are sociable; but he is different. He has great gifts, Samuel has.'

The meal over, we went up on the roof to smoke our cigars in the open air; when the sun had disappeared and his glory had darkened into twilight, our host joined us. He was a tall man, wasted and gaunt, with piercing dark eyes and dark hair, tinged with gray; hanging down upon his shoulders. (Why is it that long hair on the outside is almost always the sign of something wrong in the inside of a man's head?) He wore a black robe like a priest's cassock, and on his head a black skull-cap like the *Faust* of the operatic stage.

'Why were the Flats called St. Clair?' I said; for there is something fascinating to me in the unknown history of the West. 'There isn't any,' do you say? you I mean, who are strong in the Punic wars! you, too, who are so well up in Grecian mythology. But there is history, only we don't know it. The story of Lake Huron in the time of the Pharaohs, the story of the Mississippi during the reign of Belshazzar, would be worth hearing. But it is lost? All we can do is to gather together the details of our era,—the era when Columbus came to this New World, which was, nevertheless, as old as the world he left behind.

'It was in 1679,' began Waiting Samuel, 'that La Salle sailed up the Detroit River in his little vessel of sixty tons burden, called the Griffin. He was accompanied by thirty-four men, mostly fur-traders; but there were among them two holy monks, and Father Louis Hennepin, a friar of the Franciscan order. They passed up the river and entered the little lake just south of us, crossing it and these Flats on the 12th of August, which is St. Clair's day. Struck with the gentle beauty of the scene, they named the waters after their saint, and at sunset sang a *Te Deum* in her honor.'

'And who was Saint Clair?'

'Saint Clair, virgin and abbess, born in Italy, in 1193, made superior of a convent by the great Francis, and canonized for her distinguished virtues,' said Samuel, as though reading from an encyclopædia.

'Are you a Roman Catholic?' asked Raymond.

'I am everything; all sincere faith is sacred to me,' replied the man. 'It is but a question of names.'

'Tell us of your religion,' said Raymond, thoughtfully; for in religions Raymond was something of a polyglot.

'You would hear of my faith? Well, so be it. Your question is the work of spirit influence. Listen, then. The great Creator has sowed immensity with innumerable systems of suns. In one of these systems a spirit forgot that he was a limited, subordinate being, and misused his freedom; how, we know not. He fell, and with him all his kind. A new race was then created for the vacant world, and, according to the fixed purpose of the Creator, each was left free to act for himself; he loves not mere machines. The fallen spirit, envying the new creature called man, tempted him to sin. What was his sin? Simply the giving up of his birthright, the divine soul-sparkle, for an earthly pleasure. The triune divine deep, the mysterious fiery triangle, which, to our finite minds, best represents the Deity, now withdrew his personal presence; the elements, their balance broken, stormed upon man; his body, which was once ethereal, moving by mere volition, now grew heavy; and it was also appointed unto him to die. The race thus darkened, crippled, and degenerate, sank almost to the level of brutes, the mind-fire alone remaining of all their spiritual gifts. They lived on blindly, and as blindly died. The sun, however, was left to them, a type of what they had lost.

'At length, in the fulness of time, the world-day of four thousand years, which was appointed by the council in heaven for the regiving of the divine and forfeited soul-sparkle, as on the fourth day of creation the great sun was given, there came to earth the earth's compassionate Saviour, who took upon himself our degenerate body, and revivified it with the divine soul-sparkle, who overcame all our temptations, and finally allowed the tinder of our sins to perish in his own painful death upon the cross. Through him our paradise body was restored, it waits for us on the other side of the grave. He showed us what it was like on Mount Tabor, with it he passed through closed doors, walked upon the water, and ruled the elements; so will it be with us. Paradise will come again; this world will, for a thousand years, see its first estate; it will be again the Garden of Eden. America is the great escaping-place; here will the change begin. As it is written, 'Those who escape to my utmost borders.' As the time draws near, the spirits who watch above are permitted to speak to those souls who listen. Of these listening, waiting souls am I; therefore have I withdrawn myself. The sun himself speaks to me, the greatest spirit of all; each morning I watch for his coming; each morning I ask, 'Is it to-day?' Thus do I wait.'

'And how long have you been waiting?' I asked.

'I know not; time is nothing to me.'

'Is the great day near at hand?' said Raymond.

'Almost at its dawning; the last days are passing.'

'How do you know this?'

'The spirits tell me. Abide here, and perhaps they will speak to you also,' replied Waiting Samuel.

We made no answer. Twilight had darkened into night, and the Flats had sunk into silence below us. After some moments I turned to speak to our host; but, noiselessly as one of his own spirits, he had departed.

'A strange mixture of Jacob Bœhmen, chiliastic dreams, Christianity, sun-worship, and modern spiritualism,' I said. 'Much learning hath made the Maine farmer mad.'

'Is he mad?' said Raymond. 'Sometimes I think we are all mad.'

'We should certainly become so if we spent our time in speculations upon subjects clearly beyond our reach. The whole race of philosophers from Plato down are all the time going round in a circle. As long as we are in the world, I for one propose to keep my feet on solid ground; especially as we have no wings. 'Abide here, and perhaps the spirits will speak to you,' did he say? I think very likely they will, and to such good purpose that you won't have any mind left.'

'After all, why should not spirits speak to us?' said Raymond, in a musing tone.

As he uttered these words the mocking laugh of a loon came across the dark waste.

'The very loons are laughing at you,' I said, rising. 'Come down; there is a chill in the air, composed in equal parts of the Flats, the night, and Waiting Samuel. Come down, man; come down to the warm kitchen and common-sense.'

We found Roxana alone by the fire, whose glow was refreshingly real and warm; it was like the touch of a flesh-and-blood hand, after vague dreamings of spirit-companions, cold and intangible at best, with the added suspicion that, after all, they are but creations of our own fancy, and even their spirit-nature fictitious. Prime, the graceful *raconteur* who goes a-fishing, says, 'firelight is as much of a polisher in-doors as moonlight outside.' It is; but with a different result. The moonlight polishes everything into romance, the firelight into comfort. We brought up two remarkably easy old chairs in front of the hearth and sat down, Raymond still adrift with his wandering thoughts, I, as usual, making talk out of the present. Roxana sat opposite, knitting in hand, the cat purring at her feet. She was a slender woman, with faded light hair, insignificant features, small dull blue eyes, and a general aspect which, with every desire to state at its best, I can only call commonplace. Her gown was limp, her hands roughened with work, and there was no collar around her yellow throat. O magic rim of white, great is thy power! With thee, man is civilized; without thee, he becomes at once a savage.

'I am out of pork,' remarked Roxana, casually; 'I must go over to the mainland to-morrow and get some.'

If it had been anything but pork! In truth, the word did not chime with the mystic conversation of Waiting Samuel. Yes; there was no doubt about it. Roxana's mind was sadly commonplace.

'See what I have found,' I said, after a while, taking out the old breastpin. 'The stone is gone; but who knows? It might have been a diamond dropped by some French duchess, exiled, and fleeing for life across these far Western waters; or perhaps that German Princess of Brunswick-Wolfen-something-or-other, who, about one hundred years ago, was dead and buried in Russia, and travelling in America at the same time, a sort of a female wandering Jew, who has been done up in stories ever since.'

(The other day, in Bret Harte's 'Melons,' I saw the following: 'The singular conflicting conditions of John Brown's body and soul were, at that time, beginning to attract the attention of American youth.' That is good, isn't it? Well, at the time I visited the Flats, the singular conflicting conditions of the Princess of Brunswick-Wolfen-something-or-other had, for a long time, haunted me.)

Roxana's small eyes were near-sighted; she peered at the empty setting, but said nothing.

'It is water-logged,' I continued, holding it up in the firelight, 'and it hath a brassy odor; nevertheless, I feel convinced that it belonged to the princess.'

Roxana leaned forward and took the trinket; I lifted up my arms and gave a mighty stretch, one of those enjoyable lengthenings-out which belong only to the healthy fatigue of country life. When I drew myself in again, I was surprised to see Roxana's features working, and her rough hands trembling, as she held the battered setting.

'It was mine,' she said; 'my dear old cameo breastpin that Abby gave me when I was married. I saved it and saved it, and wouldn't sell it, no matter how low we got, for someway it seemed to tie me to home and baby's grave. I used to wear it when I had baby—I had neck-ribbons then; we had things like other folks, and on Sundays we went to the old meeting-house on the green. Baby is buried there—O baby, baby!' and the voice broke into sobs.

'You lost a child?' I said, pitying the sorrow which was, which must be, so lonely, so unshared.

'Yes. O baby! baby!' cried the woman, in a wailing tone. 'It was a little boy, gentlemen, and it had curly hair, and could just talk a word or two; its name was Ethan, after father, but we all called it Robin. Father was mighty proud of Robin, and mother, too. It died, gentlemen, my baby died, and I buried it in the old churchyard near the thorn-tree. But still I thought to stay there always along with mother and the girls; I never supposed anything else, until Samuel began to see visions. Then, everything was different, and everybody against us; for, you see, I would marry Samuel, and when he left off working and began to talk to the spirits, the folks all said, 'I told yer so, Maria Ann!' Samuel wasn't of Maine stock exactly: his father was a sailor, and 't was suspected that his mother was some kind of an East-Injia woman, but no one knew. His father died and left the boy on the town, so he lived round from house to house until he got old enough to hire out. Then he came to our farm, and there he stayed. He had wonderful eyes, Samuel had, and he had a way with him—well, the long and short of it was, that I got to thinking about him, and couldn't think of anything else. The folks didn't like it at all, for, you see, there was Adam Rand, who had a farm of his own over the hill; but I never could bear Adam Rand. The worst of it was, though, that Samuel never so much as looked at me, hardly. Well, it got to be the second year, and Susan, my younger sister, married Adam Rand. Adam, he thought he'd break up my nonsense, that's what they called it, and so he got a good place for Samuel away down in Connecticut, and Samuel said he'd go, for he was always restless, Samuel was. When I heard it, I was ready to lie down and die. I ran out into the pasture and threw myself down by the fence like a crazy woman. Samuel happened to come by along the lane, and saw me; he was always kind to all the dumb creatures, and stopped to see what was the matter, just as he would have stopped to help a calf. It all came out then, and he was awful sorry for me. He sat down on the top bar of the fence and looked at me, and I sat on the ground a-crying with my hair down, and my face all red and swollen.

'I never thought to marry, Maria Ann,' says he.

'O, please do, Samuel,' says I, 'I'm a real good housekeeper, I am, and we can have a little land of our own, and everything nice—'

'But I wanted to go away. My father was a sailor,' he began, a-looking off toward the ocean.

'O, I can't stand it,' says I, beginning to cry again. Well after that he 'greed to stay at home and marry me, and the folks they had to give in to it when they saw how I felt. We were married on Thanksgiving day, and I wore a pink delaine, purple neck-ribbon, and this very breastpin that sister Abby gave me,—it cost four dollars, and came 'way from Boston. Mother kissed me, and said she hoped I'd be happy.

'Of course I shall, mother,' says I, 'Samuel has great gifts; he isn't like common folks.'

'But common folks is a deal comfortabler,' says mother. The folks never understood Samuel.

'Well, we had a chirk little house and bit of land, and baby came, and was so cunning and pretty. The visions had begun to appear then, and Samuel said he must go.

'Where?' says I.

'Anywhere the spirits lead me,' says he.

'But baby couldn't travel, and so it hung along; Samuel left off work, and everything ran down to loose ends; I did the best I could, but it wasn't much. Then baby died, and I buried him under the thorn-tree, and the visions came thicker and thicker; Samuel told me as how this time he must go. The folks wanted me to stay behind without him; but they never understood me nor him. I could no more leave him than I could fly; I was just wrapped up in him. So we went away; I cried dreadfully when it came to leaving the folks and Robin's little grave, but I had so much to do after we got started, that there wasn't time for anything but work. We thought to settle in ever so many places, but after a while there would always come a vision, and I'd have to sell out and start on. The little money we had was soon gone, and then I went out for days' work, and picked up any work I could get. But many's the time we were cold, and many's the time we were hungry, gentlemen. The visions kept coming, and by and by I got to like 'em too. Samuel he told me all they said when I came home nights, and it was nice to hear all about the thousand years of joy, when there'd be no more trouble, and when Robin would come back to us again. Only I told Samuel that I hoped the world wouldn't alter much, because I wanted to go back to Maine for a few days, and see all the old places. Father and mother are dead, I suppose,' said Roxana, looking up at us with a pathetic expression in her small dull eyes. Beautiful eyes are doubly beautiful in sorrow; but there is something peculiarly pathetic in small dull eyes looking up at you, struggling to express the grief that lies within, like a prisoner behind the bars of his small dull window.

'And how did you lose your breastpin?' I said, coming back to the original subject.

'Samuel found I had it, and threw it away soon after we came to the Flats; he said it was vanity.'

'Have you been here long?'

'O yes, years. I hope we shall stay here always now,—at least, I mean until the thousand years of joy begin,—for it's quiet, and Samuel's more easy here than in any other place. I've got used to the lonely feeling, and don't mind it much now. There's no one near us for miles, Rosabel Lee and Liakim; they don't come here, for Samuel can't abide 'em, but sometimes I stop there on my way over from the mainland, and have a little chat about the children. Rosabel Lee has got lovely children, she has! They don't stay there in the winter, though; the winters *are* long, I don't deny it.'

'What do you do then?'

'Well, I knit and cook, and Samuel reads to me, and has a great many visions.'

'He has books, then!'

'Yes, all kinds; he's a great reader, and he has boxes of books about the spirits, and such things.'

'Nine of the night. Take thou thy rest. I will lay me down in peace and sleep, for it is thou, Lord, that makest me dwell in safety,' chanted the voice in the hall; and our evening was over.

At dawn we attended the service on the roof; then, after breakfast, we released Captain Kidd, and started out for another day's sport. We had not rowed far when Roxana passed us, poling her flat-boat rapidly along; she had a load of fish and butter, and was bound for the mainland village. 'Bring us back a Detroit paper,' I said. She nodded and passed on, stolid and homely in the morning light. Yes, I was obliged to confess to myself that she *was* commonplace.

A glorious day we had on the moors in the rushing September wind. Everything rustled and waved and danced, and the grass undulated in long billows as far as the eye could see. The wind enjoyed himself like mad; he had no forests to oppose him, no heavy water to roll up,—nothing but merry, swaying grasses. It was the west wind,—'of all the winds, the best wind.'

The east wind was given us for our sins; I have long suspected that the east wind was the angel that drove Adam out of Paradise. We did nothing that day,—nothing but enjoy the rushing breeze. We felt like Bedouins of the desert, with our boat for a steed. 'He came flying upon the wings of the wind,' is the grandest image of the Hebrew poet.

Late in the afternoon we heard the bugle and returned, following our clew as before. Roxana had brought a late paper, and, opening it, I saw the account of an accident,—a yacht run down on the Sound and five drowned; five, all near and dear to us. Hastily and sadly we gathered our possessions together; the hunting, the fishing, were nothing now; all we thought of was to get away, to go home to the sorrowing ones around the new-made graves. Roxana went with us in her boat to guide us back to the little lighthouse. Waiting Samuel bade us no farewell, but as we rowed away we saw him standing on the house-top gazing after us. We bowed; he waved his hand; and then turned away to look at the sunset. What were our little affairs to a man who held converse with the spirits!

We rowed in silence. How long, how weary seemed the way! The grasses, the lilies, the silver channels,—we no longer even saw them. At length the forward boat stopped. 'There's the lighthouse yonder,' said Roxana. 'I won't go over there to-night. Mayhap you'd rather not talk, and Rosabel Lee will be sure to talk to me. Good by.' We shook hands, and I laid in the boat a sum of money to help the little household through the winter; then we rowed on toward the lighthouse. At the turn I looked back; Roxana was sitting motionless in her boat; the dark clouds were rolling up behind her; and the Flats looked wild and desolate. 'God help her!' I said.

A steamer passed the lighthouse and took us off within the hour.

Years rolled away, and I often thought of the grassy sea, and its singularly strange associations, and intended to go there; but the intention never grew into reality. In 1870, however, I was travelling westward, and, finding myself at Detroit, a sudden impulse took me up to the Flats. The steamer sailed up the beautiful river and crossed the little lake, both unchanged. But, alas! the canal predicted by the captain fifteen years before had been cut, and, in all its unmitigated ugliness, stretched straight through the enchanted land. I got off at the new and prosaic brick lighthouse, half expecting to see Liakim and his Rosabel Lee; but they were not there, and no one knew anything about them. And Waiting Samuel? No one knew anything about him either. I took a skiff, and, at the risk of losing myself, I rowed away into the wilderness, spending the day among the silvery channels, which were as beautiful as ever. There were fewer birds; I saw no grave herons, no sombre bitterns, and the fish had grown shy. But the water-lilies were beautiful as of old, and the grasses as delicate and luxuriant. I had scarcely a hope of finding the old house on the island, but late in the afternoon, by a mere chance, I rowed up unexpectedly to its little landing-place. The walls stood firm and the roof unbroken; I landed and walked up the overgrown path. Opening the door, I found the few old chairs and tables in their places, weather-beaten and decayed, the storms had forced a way within, and the floor was insecure; but the gay crockery was on its shelf, the old tins against the wall, and all looked so natural that I almost feared to find the mortal remains of the husband and wife as I went from room to room. They were not there, however, and the place looked as if it had been uninhabited for years. I lingered in the doorway. What had become of them? Were they dead? Or had a new vision sent them farther toward the setting sun? I never knew, although I made many inquiries. If dead, they were probably lying somewhere under the shining waters; if alive, they must have 'folded their tents, like the Arabs, and silently stolen away.'

I rowed back in the glow of the evening across the grassy sea. 'It is beautiful, beautiful,' I thought, 'but it is passing away. Already commerce has invaded its borders; a few more years and its loveliness will be but a legend of the past. The bittern has vanished; the loon has fled away. Waiting Samuel was the prophet of the waste; he has gone, and the barriers are broken down. No artist has painted, no poet has sung your wild, vanishing charm; but in one heart, at least, you have a place, O lovely land of St. Clair!'

THE LADY OF LITTLE FISHING

IT was an island in Lake Superior.

I beached my canoe there about four o'clock in the afternoon, for the wind was against me and a high sea running. The late summer of 1850, and I was coasting along the south shore of the great lake, hunting, fishing, and camping on the beach, under the delusion that in that way I was living 'close to the great heart of nature,'—whatever that may mean. Lord Bacon got up the phrase; I suppose he knew. Pulling the boat high and dry on the sand with the comfortable reflection that here were no tides to disturb her with their goings-out and comings-in, I strolled through the woods on a tour of exploration, expecting to find bluebells, Indian pipes, juniper rings, perhaps a few agates along-shore, possibly a bird or two for company. I found a town.

It was deserted; but none the less a town, with three streets, residences, a meeting-house, gardens, a little park, and an attempt at a fountain. Ruins are rare in the New World. I took off my hat. 'Hail, homes of the past!' I said. (I cultivated the habit of thinking aloud when I was living close to the great heart of nature.) 'A human voice resounds through your arches' (there were no arches,—logs won't arch; but never mind) 'once more, a human hand touches your venerable walls, a human foot presses your deserted hearth-stones.' I then selected the best half of the meeting-house for a camp, and kindled a glorious bonfire in the park. 'Now that you are illuminated with joy, O Ruin,' I remarked, 'I will go down to the beach and bring up my supplies. It is long since I have had a roof over my head; I promise you to stay until your last residence is well burned; then I will make a final cup of coffee with the meeting-house itself, and depart in peace, leaving your poor old bones buried in decent ashes.'

The ruin made no objection, and I took up my abode there, the roof of the meeting-house was still water-tight (which is an advantage when the great heart of nature grows wet). I kindled a fire on the sacerdotal hearth, cooked my supper, ate it in leisurely comfort, and then stretched myself on a blanket to enjoy an evening pipe of peace, listening meanwhile to the sounding of the wind through the great pine-trees. There was no door to my sanctuary, but I had the cosey far end; the island was uninhabited, there was not a boat in sight at sunset, nothing could disturb me unless it might be a ghost. Presently a ghost came in.

It did not wear the traditional gray tarlatan armor of Hamlet's father, the only ghost with whom I am well acquainted; this spectre was clad in substantial deer-skin garments, and carried a gun and loaded game-bag. It came forward to my hearth, hung up its gun, opened its game-bag, took out some birds, and inspected them gravely.

'Fat?' I inquired.

'They'll do,' replied the spectre, and forthwith set to work preparing them for the coals. I smoked on in silence. The spectre seemed to be a skilled cook, and after deftly broiling its supper, it offered me a share; I accepted. It swallowed a huge mouthful and crunched with its teeth; the spell was broken, and I knew it for a man of flesh and blood.

He gave his name as Reuben, and proved himself an excellent camping companion; in fact, he shot all the game, caught all the fish, made all the fires, and cooked all the food for us both. I proposed to him to stay and help me burn up the ruin, with the condition that when the last timber of the meeting-house was consumed, we should shake hands and depart, one to the east, one to the west, without a backward glance. 'In that way we shall not infringe upon each other's personality,' I said.

'Agreed,' replied Reuben.

He was a man of between fifty and sixty years, while I was on the sunny side of thirty; he was reserved, I was always generously affable; he was an excellent cook, while I—well, I wasn't; he was taciturn, and so, in payment for the work he did, I entertained him with conversation, or rather monologue, in my most brilliant style. It took only two weeks to burn up the town, burned we never so slowly; at last it came to the meeting house, which now stood by itself in the vacant clearing. It was a cool September day; we cooked breakfast with the roof, dinner with the sides, supper with the odds and ends, and then applied a torch to the framework. Our last camp-fire was a glorious one. We lay stretched on our blankets, smoking and watching the glow. 'I wonder, now, who built the old shanty,' I said in a musing tone.

'Well,' replied Reuben, slowly, 'if you really want to know, I will tell you. I did.'

'You!'

'Yes.'

'You didn't do it alone?'

'No; there were about forty of us.'

'Here?'

'Yes; here at Little Fishing;'

'Little Fishing?'

'Yes; Little Fishing Island. That is the name of the place.'

'How long ago was this?'

'Thirty years.'

'Hunting and trapping, I suppose?'

'Yes; for the Northwest and Hudson Bay Companies.'

'Wasn't a meeting house an unusual accompaniment?'

'Most unusual.'

'Accounted for in this case by—'

'A woman.'

'Ah!' I said in a tone of relish; 'then of course there is a story?'

'There is.'

'Out with it, comrade. I scarcely expected to find the woman and her story up here; but since the irrepressible creature would come, out with her by all means. She shall grace our last pipe together, the last timber of our meeting-house, our last night on Little Fishing. The dawn will see us far from each other, to meet no more this side heaven. Speak then, O comrade mine! I am in one of my rare listening moods!'

I stretched myself at ease and waited. Reuben was a long time beginning but I was too indolent to urge him. At length he spoke.

'They were a rough set here at Little Fishing, all the worse for being all white men; most of the other camps were full of half-breeds and Indians. The island had been a station away back in the early days of the Hudson Bay Company; it was a station for the Northwest Company while that lasted; then it went back to the Hudson, and stayed there until the company moved its forces farther to the north. It was not at any time a regular post; only a camp for the hunters. The post was farther down the lake. O, but those were wild days! You think you know the wilderness, boy; but you know nothing, absolutely nothing. It makes me laugh to see the airs of you city gentlemen with your fine guns, improved fishing-tackle, elaborate paraphernalia, as though you were going to wed the whole forest, floating up and down the lake for a month or two in the summer! You should have seen the hunters of Little Fishing going out gayly when the mercury was down twenty degrees below zero, for a week in the woods. You should have seen the trappers wading through the hard snow, breast high, in the gray dawn, visiting the traps and hauling home the prey. There were all kinds of men here, Scotch, French, English, and American; all classes, the high and the low, the educated and the ignorant; all sorts, the lazy and the hard-working. One thing only they all had in common,—badness. Some had fled to the wilderness to escape the law, others to escape order; some had chosen the wild life because of its wildness, others had drifted into it from sheer lethargy. This far northern border did not attract the plodding emigrant, the respectable settler. Little Fishing held none of that trash; only a reckless set of fellows who carried their lives in their hands, and tossed them up, if need be without a second thought.'

'And other people's lives without a third,' I suggested.

'Yes; if they deserved it. But nobody whined; there wasn't any nonsense here. The men went hunting and trapping, got the furs ready for the bateaux, ate when they were hungry, drank when they were thirsty, slept when they were sleepy, played cards when they felt like it, and got angry and knocked each other down whenever they chose. As I said before, there wasn't any nonsense at Little Fishing,—until *she* came.'

'Ah! the she!'

'Yes, the Lady,—our Lady, as we called her. Thirty-one years ago; how long it seems!'

'And well it may,' I said. 'Why, comrade, I wasn't born then!'

This stupendous fact seemed to strike me more than my companion; he went on with his story as though I had not spoken.

'One October evening, four of the boys had got into a row over the cards; the rest of us had come out of our wigwams to see the fun, and were sitting around on the stumps, chaffing them, and laughing; the camp-fire was burning in front, lighting up the woods with a red glow for a short distance, and making the rest doubly black all around. There we were, as I said before, quite easy and comfortable, when suddenly there appeared among us, as though she had dropped from heaven, a woman!

'She was tall and slender, the firelight shone full on her pale face and dove-colored dress, her golden hair was folded back under a little white cap, and a white kerchief lay over her shoulders; she looked spotless. I stared; I could scarcely believe my eyes; none of us could. There was not a white woman west of the Sault Ste. Marie. The four fellows at the table sat as if transfixed; one had his partner by the throat, the other two were disputing over a point in the game. The lily lady glided up to their table, gathered the cards in her white hands, slowly, steadily, without pause or trepidation before their astonished eyes, and then, coming back, she threw the cards into the centre of the glowing fire. 'Ye shall not play away your souls,' she said in a clear, sweet voice. 'Is not the game sin? And its reward death?' And then, immediately, she gave us a sermon, the like of which was never heard before; no argument, no doctrine, just simple, pure entreaty. 'For the love of God,' she ended, stretching out her hands toward our silent, gazing group,—'for the love of God, my brothers, try to do better.'

'We did try; but it was not for the love of God. Neither did any of us feel like brothers.

'She did not give any name; we called her simply our Lady, and she accepted the title. A bundle carefully packed in birch-bark was found on the beach. 'Is this yours?' asked black Andy.

'It is,' replied the Lady; and removing his hat, the black-haired giant carried the package reverently inside her lodge. For we had given her our best wigwam, and fenced it off with pine saplings so that it looked like a miniature fortress. The Lady did not suggest this stockade; it was our own idea, and with one accord we worked at it like beavers, and hung up a gate with a ponderous bolt inside.

'Mais, ze can nevare farsen eet wiz her leetle fingares,' said Frenchy, a sallow little wretch with a turn for handicraft; so he contrived a small spring which shot the bolt into place with a touch. The Lady lived in her fortress; three times a day the men carried food to her door, and, after tapping gently, withdrew again, stumbling over each other in their haste. The Flying Dutchman, a stolid Holland-born sailor, was our best cook, and the pans and kettles were generally left to him; but now all wanted to try their skill, and the results were extraordinary.

'She's never touched that pudding, now' said Nightingale Jack, discontentedly, as his concoction of berries and paste came back from the fortress door.

'She will starve soon, I think,' remarked the Doctor, calmly; 'to my certain knowledge she has not had an eatable meal for four days.' And he lighted a fresh pipe. This was an aside, and the men pretended not to hear it; but the pans were relinquished to the Dutchman from that time forth.

'The Lady wore always her dove-colored robe, and little white cap, through whose muslin we could see the glimmer of her golden hair. She came and went among us like a spirit; she knew no fear; she turned our life inside out, nor shrank from its vileness. It seemed as though she was not of earth, so utterly impersonal was her interest in us, so heavenly her pity. She took up our sins, one by one, as an angel might; she pleaded with us for our own lost souls, she spared us not, she held not back one grain of denunciation, one iota of future punishment. Sometimes, for days, we would not see her; then, at twilight, she would glide out among us, and, standing in the light of the camp-fire, she would preach to us as though inspired. We listened to her; I do not mean that we were one whit better at heart, but still we listened to her, always. It was a wonderful sight, that lily face under the pine-trees, that spotless woman standing alone in the glare of the fire, while around her lay forty evil-minded, lawless men, not one of whom but would have killed his neighbor for so much as a disrespectful thought of her.

'So strange was her coming, so almost supernatural her appearance in this far forest, that we never wondered over its cause, but simply accepted it as a sort of miracle; your thoroughly irreligious men are always superstitious. Not one of us would have asked a question, and we should never have known her story had she not herself told it to us; not immediately, not as though it was of any importance, but quietly, briefly, and candidly as a child. She came, she said, from Scotland, with a band of God's people. She had always been in one house, a religious institution of some kind, sewing for the poor when her strength allowed it, but generally ill, and suffering much from pain in her head; often kept under the influence of soothing medicines for days together. She had no father or mother, she was only one of this band; and when they decided to send out missionaries to America, she begged to go, although but a burden; the sea voyage restored her health; she grew, she said, in strength and in grace, and her heart was as the heart of a lion. Word came to her from on high that she should come up into the northern lake-country and preach the gospel there; the band were going to the verdant prairies. She left them in the night, taking nothing but her clothing; a friendly vessel carried her north; she had preached the gospel everywhere. At the Sault the priests had driven her out, but nothing fearing, she went on into the wilderness, and so, coming part of the way in canoes, part of the way along-shore, she had reached our far island. Marvellous kindness had she met with, she said; the Indians, the half-breeds, the hunters, and the trappers had all received her, and helped her on her way from camp to camp. They had listened to her words also. At Portage they had begged her to stay through the winter, and offered to build her a little church for Sunday services. Our men looked at each other. Portage was the worst camp on the lake, notorious for its fights; it was a mining settlement.

'But I told them I must journey on toward the west,' continued our Lady. 'I am called to visit every camp on this shore before winter sets in; I must soon leave you also.'

'The men looked at each other again; the Doctor was spokesman. 'But, my Lady,' he said 'the next post is Fort William, two hundred and thirty-five miles away on the north shore.'

'It is almost November; the snow will soon be six and ten feet deep. The Lady could never travel through it,—could she now?' said Black Andy, who had begun eagerly, but in his embarrassment at the sound of his own voice, now turned to Frenchy and kicked him covertly into answering.

'Nevare!' replied the Frenchman; he had intended to place his hand upon his heart to give emphasis to his word, but the Lady turned her calm eyes that way, and his grimy paw fell, its gallantry wilted.

'I thought there was one more camp,—at Burntwood River,' said our Lady in a musing tone. The men looked at each other a third time; there was a camp there, and they all knew it. But the Doctor was equal to the emergency.

'That camp, my Lady,' he said gravely,—'that camp no longer exists! Then he whispered hurriedly to the rest of us, 'It will be an easy job to clean it out, boys. We'll send over a party to-night; it's only thirty-five miles.'

'We recognized superior genius; the Doctor was our oldest and deepest sinner. But what struck us most was his anxiety to make good his lie. Had it then come to this,—that the Doctor told the truth?

'The next day we all went to work to build our Lady a church; in a week it was completed. There goes its last cross-beam now into the fire; it was a solid piece of work, wasn't it? It has stood this climate thirty years. I remember the first Sunday service: we all washed, and dressed ourselves in the best we had; we scarcely knew each other we were so fine. The Lady was pleased with the church, but yet she had not said she would stay all winter; we were still anxious. How she preached to us that day! We had made a screen of young spruces set in boxes, and her figure stood out against the dark green background like a thing of light. Her silvery voice rang through the log-temple, her face seemed to us like a star. She had no color in her cheeks at any time; her dress, too, was colorless. Although gentle, there was an iron inflexibility about her slight, erect form. We felt, as we saw her standing there, that if need be she would walk up to the cannon's mouth, with a smile. She took a little book from her pocket and read to us a hymn,—'O come, all ye faithful,' the old 'Adeste Fideles.' Some of us knew it; she sang, and gradually, shamefacedly, voices joined in. It was a sight to see Nightingale Jack solemnly singing away about 'choirs of angels'; but it was a treat to hear him, too,—what a voice he had! Then our Lady prayed, kneeling down on the little platform in front of the evergreens, clasping her hands, and lifting her eyes to heaven. We did not know what to do at first, but the Doctor gave us a severe look and bent his head, and we all followed his lead.

'When service was over and the door opened, we found that it had been snowing; we could not see out through the windows because white cloth was nailed over them in place of glass.

'"Now, my Lady, you will have to stay with us," said the Doctor. We all gathered around with eager faces.

'"Do you really believe that it will be for the good of your souls?" asked the sweet voice.

'The Doctor believed—for us all.

'"Do you really hope?"

'The Doctor hoped.

'"Will you try to do your best?"

'The Doctor was sure he would.

'"I will," answered the Flying Dutchman, earnestly. "I moost not fry de meat any more; I moost broil!"

'For we had begged him for months to broil, and he had obstinately refused; broil represented the good, and fry the evil, to his mind; he came out for the good according to his light; but none the less did we fall upon him behind the Lady's back, and cuff him into silence.

'She stayed with us all winter. You don't know what the winters are up here; steady, bitter cold for seven months, thermometer always below, the snow dry as dust, the air like a knife. We built a compact chimney for our Lady, and we cut cords of wood into small, light sticks, easy for her to lift, and stacked them in her shed; we lined her lodge with skins, and we made oil from bear's fat and rigged up a kind of lamp for her. We tried to make candles, I remember, but they would not run straight; they came out humpbacked and sidling, and burned themselves to wick in no time. Then we took to improving the town. We had lived in all kinds of huts and lean-to shanties; now nothing would do but regular log-houses. If it had been summer, I don't know what we might not have run to in the way of piazzas and fancy steps; but with the snow five feet deep, all we could accomplish was a plain, square log-house, and even that took our whole force. The only way to keep the peace was to have all the houses exactly alike; we laid out the three streets, and built the houses, all facing the meeting-house, just as you found them.'

'And where was the Lady's lodge?' I asked, for I recalled no stockaded fortress, large or small.

My companion hesitated a moment. Then he said abruptly, 'it was torn down.'

'Torn down!' I repeated. 'Why, what—'

Reuben waved his hand with a gesture that silenced me, and went on with his story. It came to me then for the first time, that he was pursuing the current of his own thoughts rather than entertaining me. I turned to look at him with a new interest. I had talked to him for two weeks, in rather a patronizing way; could it be that affairs were now, at this moment, reversed?

'It took us almost all winter to build those houses,' pursued Reuben. 'At one time we neglected the hunting and trapping to such a degree, that the Doctor called a meeting and expressed his opinion. Ours was a voluntary camp, in a measure, but still we had formally agreed to get a certain amount of skins ready for the bateaux by early spring; this agreement was about the only real bond of union between us. Those whose houses were not completed scowled at the Doctor.

'"Do you suppose I'm going to live like an Injun when the other fellows has regular houses?" inquired Black Andy, with a menacing air.

'"By no means," replied the Doctor, blandly, "My plan is this: build at night."

'"At night?"

'"Yes; by the light of pine fires."

'We did. After that, we faithfully went out hunting and trapping as long as daylight lasted, and then, after supper, we built up huge fires of pine logs, and went to work on the next house. It was a strange picture; the forest deep in snow, black with night, the red glow of the great fires, and our moving figures working on as complacently as though daylight, balmy air, and the best of tools were ours.

'The Lady liked our industry. She said our new houses showed that the "new cleanliness of our inner man required a cleaner tabernacle for the outer." I don't know about our inner man, but our outer was certainly much cleaner.

'One day the Flying Dutchman made one of his unfortunate remarks. "De boys t'inks you'll like dem better in nize houses," he announced when, happening to pass the fortress, he found the Lady standing at her gate gazing at the work of the preceding night. Several of the men were near enough to hear him, but too far off to kick him into silence as usual; but they glared at him instead. The Lady looked at the speaker with her dreamy, far-off eyes.

'"De boys t'inks you like dem," began the Dutchman again, thinking she did not comprehend; but at that instant he caught the combined glare of the six eyes, and stopped abruptly, not all knowing what was wrong, but sure there was something.

'"Like them," repeated the Lady, dreamily; "yea I do like them. Nay, more, I love them. Their souls are as dear to me as the souls of brothers."

'Say, Frenchy, have you got a sister?' said Nightingale Jack, confidentially, that evening.

'Mais oui,' said Frenchy.

'You think all creation of her, I suppose?'

'We fight like four cats and one dog; *she* is the cats,' said the Frenchman concisely.

'You don't say so!' replied Jack. 'Now, I never had a sister,—but I thought perhaps—' He paused, and the sentence remained unfinished.

'The Nightingale and I were housemates. We sat late over our fire not long after that; I gave a gigantic yawn. 'This lifting logs half the night is enough to kill one,' I said, getting out my jug. Sing something, Jack. It's a long time since I've heard anything but hymns.'

'Jack always went off as easily as a music-box: you only had to wind him up; the jug was the key. I soon had him in full blast. He was giving out

'The minute gun at sea,—the minute gun at sea,'

with all the pathos of his tenor voice, when the door burst open and the whole population rushed in upon us.

'What do you mean by shouting thes way, in the middle of the night?'

'Shut up your howling, Jack.'

'How do you suppose any one can sleep?'

'It's a disgrace to the camp!'

'Now then, gentlemen,' I replied, for my blood was up (whiskey, perhaps), 'is this my house, or isn't it? If I want music, I'll have it. Time was when you were not so particular.'

'It was the first word of rebellion. The men looked at each other, then at me.

'I'll go and ask her if she objects,' I continued, boldly.

'No, no. You shall not.'

'Let him go,' said the Doctor, who stood smoking his pipe on the outskirts of the crowd. 'It is just as well to have that point settled now. The Minute Gun at Sea is a good moral song in its way,—a sort of marine missionary affair.'

'So I started, the others followed; we all knew that the Lady watched late; we often saw the glimmer of her lamp far on toward morning. It was burning now. The gate was fastened, I knocked; no answer. I knocked again, and yet a third time; still silence. The men stood off at a little distance and waited. 'She shall answer,' I said angrily, and going around to the side where the stockade came nearer to the wall of the lodge, I knocked loudly on the close-set saplings. For answer I thought I heard a low moan; I listened, it came again. My anger vanished, and with a mighty bound I swung myself up to the top of the stockade, sprung down inside, ran around, and tried the door. It was fastened; I burst it open and entered. There, by the light of the hanging lamp, I saw the Lady on the floor, apparently dead. I raised her in my arms; her heart was beating faintly, but she was unconscious. I had seen many fainting fits; this was something different; the limbs were rigid. I laid her on the low couch, loosened her dress, bathed her head and face in cold water, and wrenched up one of the warm hearth-stones to apply to her feet. I did not hesitate; I saw that it was a dangerous case, something like a trance or an 'ectasis.' Somebody must attend to her, and there were only men to choose from. Then why not I?

'I heard the others talking outside; they could not understand the delay; but I never heeded, and kept on my work. To tell the truth, I had studied medicine, and felt a genuine enthusiasm over a rare case. Once my patient opened her eyes and looked at me, then she lapsed away again into unconsciousness in spite of all my efforts. At last the men outside came in, angry and suspicious; they had broken down the gate. There we all stood, the whole forty of us, around the deathlike form of our Lady.

'What a night it was! To give her air, the men camped outside in the snow with a line of pickets in whispering distance from each other from the bed to their anxious group. Two were detailed to help me,—the Doctor (whose title was a sarcastic D. D.) and Jimmy, a gentle little man, excellent at bandaging broken limbs. Every vial in the camp was brought in,—astonishing lotions, drops, and balms; each man produced something; they did their best, poor fellows, and wore out the night with their anxiety. At dawn our Lady revived suddenly, thanked us all, and assured us that she felt quite well again; the trance was over. 'It was my old enemy,' she said, 'the old illness of Scotland, which I hoped had left me for ever. But I am thankful that it is no worse; I have come out of it with a clear brain. Sing a hymn of thankfulness for me, dear friends, before you go.'

'Now, we sang on Sunday in the church; but then she led us, and we had a kind of an idea that after all she did not hear us. But now, who was to lead us? We stood awkwardly around the bed, and shuffled our hats in our uneasy fingers. The Doctor fixed his eyes upon the Nightingale; Jack saw it and cowered. 'Begin,' said the Doctor in a soft voice; but gripping him in the back at the same time with an ominous clutch.

'I don't know the words,' faltered the unhappy Nightingale.

"'Now thank we all our God,
With hearts and hands and voices,'

began the Doctor, and repeated Luther's hymn with perfect accuracy from beginning to end. 'What will happen next? The Doctor knows hymns!' we thought in profound astonishment. But the Nightingale had begun, and gradually our singers joined in; I doubt whether the grand old choral was ever sung by such a company before or since. There was never any further question, by the way, about that minute gun at sea; it stayed at sea as far as we were concerned.

'Spring came, the faltering spring of Lake Superior. I won't go into my own story, but such as it was, the spring brought it back to me with new force. I wanted to go,—and yet I didn't. 'Where,' do you ask? To see her, of course,—a woman, the most beautiful,—well, never mind all that. To be brief, I loved her; she scorned me; I thought I had learned to hate her—but—I wasn't sure about it now. I kept myself aloof from the others and gave up my heart to the old sweet, bitter memories; I did not even go to church on Sundays. But all the rest went; our Lady's influence was as great as ever. I could hear them singing; they sang better now that they could have the door open; the pent-up feeling used to stifle them. The time for the bateaux drew near, and I noticed that several of the men were hard at work packing the furs in bales, a job usually left to the *voyageurs* who came with the boats. 'What's that for?' I asked.

'You don't suppose we're going to have those bateaux rascals camping on Little Fishing, do you?' said black Andy, scornfully. 'Where are your wits, Reub?'

'And they packed every skin, rafted them all over to the mainland, and waited there patiently for days, until the train of slow boats came along and took off the bales; then they came back in triumph. 'Now we're secure for another six months,' they said, and began to lay out a park, and gardens for every house. The Lady was fond of flowers; the whole town burst into blossom. The Lady liked green grass; all the clearing was soon tufted over like a lawn. The men tried the ice-cold lake every day, waiting anxiously for the time when they could bathe. There was no end to their cleanliness; Black Andy had grown almost white again, and Frenchy's hair shone like oiled silk.

'The Lady stayed on, and all went well. But, gradually, there came a discovery. The Lady was changing,—had changed! Gradually, slowly, but none the less distinctly to the eyes that knew her every eyelash. A little more hair was visible over the white brow; there was a faint color in the cheeks, a quicker step; the clear eyes were sometimes downcast now, the steady voice softer, the words at times faltering. In the early summer the white cap vanished, and she stood among us crowned only with her golden hair; one day she was seen through her open door sewing on a white robe! The men noted all these things silently; they were even a little troubled as at something they did not understand, something beyond their reach. Was she planning to leave them?

'It's my belief she's getting ready to ascend right up into heaven,' said Salem.

'Salem was a little 'wanting,' as it is called, and the men knew it; still, his words made an impression. They watched the Lady with an awe which was almost superstitious; they were troubled, and knew not why. But the Lady bloomed on. I did not pay much attention to all this; but I could not help hearing it. My heart was moody, full of its own sorrows; I secluded myself more and more. Gradually I took to going off into the mainland forests for days on solitary hunting expeditions. The camp went on its way rejoicing; the men succeeded, after a world of trouble, in making a fountain which actually played, and they glorified themselves exceedingly. The life grew quite pastoral. There was talk of importing a cow from the East, and a messenger was sent to the Sault for certain choice supplies against the coming winter. But, in the late summers the whisper went round again that the Lady had changed, this time for the worse. She looked ill, she drooped from day to day; the new life that had come to her vanished, but her former life was not restored. She grew silent and sad, she strayed away by herself through the woods, she scarcely noticed the men who followed her with anxious eyes. Time passed, and brought with it an undercurrent of trouble, suspicion, and anger. Everything went on as before; not one habit, not one custom was altered; both sides seemed to shrink from the first change, however slight. The daily life of the camp was outwardly the same, but brooding trouble filled every heart. There was no open discussion, men talked apart in twos and threes; a gloom rested over everything, but no one said, 'What is the matter?'

'There was a man among us,—I have not said much of the individual characters of our party, but this man was one of the least esteemed, or rather liked; there was not much esteem of any kind at Little Fishing. Little was known about him; although the youngest man in the camp, he was a mooning, brooding creature, with brown hair and eyes and a melancholy face. He wasn't hearty and whole-souled, and yet he wasn't an out-and-out rascal; he wasn't a leader, and yet he wasn't follower either. He wouldn't be; he was like a third horse, always. There was no goodness about him; don't go to fancying that that was the reason the men did not like him, he was as bad as they were, every inch! He never shirked his work, and they couldn't get a handle on him anywhere; but he was just—unpopular. The why and the wherefore are of no consequence now. Well, do you know what was the suspicion that hovered over the camp? It was this: our Lady loved that man!

'It took three months for all to see it, and yet never a word was spoken. All saw, all heard; but they might have been blind and deaf for any sign they gave. And the Lady drooped more and more.

'September came, the fifteenth; the Lady lay on her couch, pale and thin; the door was open and a bell stood beside her, but there was no line of pickets whispering tidings of her state to an anxious group outside. The turf in the three streets had grown yellow for want of water, the flowers in the little gardens had drooped and died, the fountain was choked with weeds, and the interiors of the houses were all untidy. It was Sunday, and near the hour for service; but the men lounged about, dingy and unwashed.

'"A'n't you going to church?" said Salem, stopping at the door of one of the houses; he was dressed in his best, with a flower in his button-hole.

'"See him now! See the fool," said Black Andy. 'He's going to church, he is! And where's the minister, Salem? Answer me that!'

'Why,—in the church, I suppose,' replied Salem, vacantly.

'"No, she a'n't; not she! She's at home, a-weeping, and a-wailing, and a-ger-nashing her teeth," replied Andy with bitter scorn.

'"What for?" said Salem.

'"What for? Why, that's the joke! Hear him, boys; he wants to know what for!"

'The loungers laughed,—a loud, reckless laugh.

'"Well, I'm going anyway," said Salem, looking wonderingly from one to the other; he passed on and entered the church.

'"I say, boys, let's have a high old time," cried Andy savagely. "Let's go back to the old way and have a jolly Sunday. Let's have out the jugs and the cards and be free again!"

'The men hesitated; ten months and more of law and order held them back.

'"What are you afraid of?" said Andy. "Not of a canting hypocrite, I hope. She's fooled us long enough, I say. Come on!" He brought out a table and stools, and produced the long-unused cards and a jug of whiskey. 'Strike up, Jack,' he cried; give us old Fiery-Eyes.'

'The Nightingale hesitated. Fiery-Eyes was a rollicking drinking song; but Andy put the glass to his lips and his scruples vanished in the tempting aroma. He began at the top of his voice, partners were chosen, and, trembling with excitement and impatience, like prisoners unexpectedly set free, the men gathered around, and made their bets.

'"What born fools we've been," said Black Andy, laying down a card.

'"Yes," replied the Flying Dutchman, "porn fools!" And he followed suit.

'But a thin white hand came down on the bits of colored pasteboard. It was our Lady. With her hair disordered, and the spots of fever in her cheeks, she stood among us again: but not as of old. Angry eyes confronted her, and Andy wrenched the cards from her grasp. "No, my Lady," he said, sternly; "never again!"

'The Lady, gazed from one face to the next, and so all around the circle; all were dark and sullen. Then she bowed her head upon her hands and wept aloud.

'There was a sudden shrinking away on all sides, the players rose, the cards were dropped. But the Lady glided away, weeping as she went; she entered the church door and the men could see her taking her accustomed place on the platform. One by one they followed; Black Andy lingered till the last, but he came. The service began, and went on falteringly, without spirit, with palpable fears of a total breaking down which never quite came; the Nightingale sang almost alone, and made sad work with the words; Salem joined in confidently, but did not improve the sense of the hymn. The Lady was silent. But when the time for the sermon came she rose and her voice burst forth.

'"Men, brothers, what have I done? A change has come over the town, a change has come over your hearts. You shun me! What have I done?"

'There was a grim silence; then the Doctor rose in his place and answered,—

'"Only this, madam. You have shown yourself to be a woman."

'"And what did you think me?"

'"A saint."

'"God forbid!" said the Lady, earnestly. "I never thought myself one."

'"I know that well. But you were a saint to us; hence your influence. It is gone."

'"Is it all gone?" asked the Lady, sadly.

'"Yes. Do not deceive yourself; we have never been one whit better save through our love for you. We held you as something high above ourselves; we were content to worship you."

'"O no, not me!" said the Lady, shuddering.

'"Yes, you, you alone! But—our idol came down among us and showed herself to be but common flesh and blood! What wonder that we stand aghast? What wonder that our hearts are bitter? What wonder (worse than all!) that when the awe has quite vanished, there is strife for the beautiful image fallen from its niche?"

'The Doctor ceased, and turned away. The Lady stretched out her hands towards the others; her face was deadly pale, and there was a bewildered expression in her eyes.

'"O, ye for whom I have prayed, for whom I have struggled to obtain a blessing,—ye whom I have loved so,—do ye desert me thus?" she cried.

'"You have deserted us," answered a voice.

'"I have not."

'"You have," cried Black Andy, pushing to the front. 'You love that Mitchell! Deny it if you dare!'

'There was an irrepressible murmur, then a sudden hush. The angry suspicion, the numbing certainty had found voice at last; the secret was out. All eyes, which had at first closed with the shock, were now fixed upon the solitary woman before them; they burned like coals.

'"Do I?" murmured the Lady, with a strange questioning look that turned from face to face,—"do I?—Great God! I do." She sank upon her knees and buried her face in her trembling hands. "The truth has come to me at last,—I do!"

'Her voice was a mere whisper, but every ear heard it, and every eye saw the crimson rise to the forehead and redden the white throat.

'For a moment there was silence, broken only by the hard breathing of the men. Then the Doctor spoke.

'"Go out and bring him in," he cried. "Bring in this Mitchell! It seems he has other things to do,—the blockhead!"

'Two of the men hurried out.

'"He shall not have her," shouted Black Andy. "My knife shall see to that!" And he pressed close to the platform. A great tumult arose, men talked angrily and clinched their fists, voices rose and fell together. "He shall not have her,—Mitchell! Mitchell!"

'"The truth is, each one of you wants her himself," said the Doctor.

'There was a sudden silence, but every man eyed his neighbor jealously. Black Andy stood in front, knife in hand, and kept guard. The Lady had not moved; she was kneeling with her face buried in her hands.

'"I wish to speak to her," said the Doctor, advancing.

'"You shall not," cried Andy, fiercely interposing.

'"You fool! I love her this moment ten thousand times more than you do. But do you suppose I would so much as touch a woman who loved another man?"

'The knife dropped; the Doctor passed on and took his place on the platform by the Lady's side. The tumult began again, for Mitchell was seen coming in the door between his two keepers.

'"Mitchell! Mitchell!" rang angrily through the church.

'"Look, woman!" said the Doctor, bending over the kneeling figure at his side. She raised her head and saw the wolfish faces below.

'"They have had ten months of your religion," he said.

'It was his revenge. Bitter, indeed; but he loved her.

'In the mean time the man Mitchell was hauled and pushed and tossed forward to the platform by rough hands that longed to throttle him on the way. At last, angry himself, but full of wonder, he confronted them, this crowd of comrades suddenly turned madmen! "What does this mean?" he asked.

'"Mean! mean!" shouted the men; "a likely story! He asks what this means!" And they laughed boisterously.

'The Doctor advanced. 'You see this woman,' he said.

'"I see our Lady."

'"Our Lady no longer; only a woman like any other,—weak and fickle. Take her,—but begone."

'"Take her!" repeated Mitchell, bewildered.—"take our Lady! And where?"

'"Fool! Liar! Blockhead!" shouted the crowd below.

'"The truth is simply this, Mitchell," continued the Doctor, quietly. "We herewith give you up our Lady,—ours no longer; for she has just confessed, openly confessed, that she loves you."

'Mitchell started back. "Loves me!"

'"Yes."

'Black Andy felt the blade of his knife. "He'll never have her alive," he muttered.

'"But," said Mitchell, bluntly confronting the Doctor, "I don't want her."

'"You don't want her?"

'"I don't love her."

'"You don't love her?"

'"Not in the least," he replied, growing angry, perhaps at himself. "What is she to me? Nothing. A very good missionary, no doubt; but *I* don't fancy woman-preachers. You may remember that *I* never gave in to her influence; *I* was never under her thumb. *I* was the only man in Little Fishing who cared nothing for her!"

'And that is the secret of *her* liking,' murmured the Doctor. 'O woman! woman! the same the world over!'

'In the mean time the crowd had stood stupefied.

'"He does not love her!" they said to each other; "he does not want her!"

'Andy's black eyes gleamed with joy; he swung himself up on to the platform. Mitchell stood there with face dark and disturbed, but he did not flinch. Whatever his faults, he was no hypocrite. 'I must leave this to-night,' he said to himself, and turned to go. But quick as a flash our Lady sprang from her knees and threw herself at his feet. 'You are going,' she cried. 'I heard what you said,—you do not love me! But take me with you! Let me be your servant—your slave—anything—anything, so that I am not parted from you, my lord and master, my only, only love!'

'She clasped his ankles with her thin, white hands, and laid her face on his dusty shoes.

'The whole audience stood dumb before this manifestation of a great love. Enraged, bitter, jealous as was each heart, there was not a man but would at that moment have sacrificed his own love that she might be blessed. Even Mitchell, in one of those rare spirit-flashes when the soul is shown bare in the lightning, asked himself, 'Can I not love her? But the soul answered, 'No.' He stooped, unclasped the clinging hands, and turned resolutely away.'

'"You are a fool," said the Doctor. 'No other woman will ever love you as she does.'

'"I know it," replied Mitchell.

'He stepped down from the platform and crossed the church, the silent crowd making a way for him as he passed along; he went out in the sunshine, through the village, down towards the beach,—they saw him no more.

'The Lady had fainted. The men bore her back to the lodge and tended her with gentle care one week,—two weeks,—three weeks. Then she died.

'They were all around her; she smiled upon them all, and called them all by name, bidding them farewell. 'Forgive me,' she whispered to the Doctor. The Nightingale sang a hymn, sang as he had never sung before. Black Andy knelt at her feet. For some minutes she lay scarcely breathing; then suddenly she opened her fading eyes. 'Friends,' she murmured, 'I am well punished. I thought myself holy,—I held myself above my kind,—but God has shown me I am the weakest of them all.'

'The next moment she was gone.

'The men buried her with tender hands. Then in a kind of blind fury against Fate, they tore down her empty lodge and destroyed its every fragment; in their grim determination they even smoothed over the ground and planted shrubs and bushes, so that the very location might be lost. But they did not stay to see the change. In a month the camp broke up of itself, the town was abandoned, and the island deserted for good and all; I doubt whether any of the men ever came back or even stopped when passing by. Probably I am the only one. Thirty years ago,—thirty years ago!'

'That Mitchell was a great fool,' I said, after a long pause. 'The Doctor was worth twenty of him; for that matter, so was Black Andy. I only hope the fellow was well punished for his stupidity.'

'He was.'

'O, you kept track of him, did you?'

'Yes. He went back into the world, and the woman he loved repulsed him a second time, and with even more scorn than before.'

'Served him right.'

'Perhaps so; but after all, what could he do? Love is not made to order. He loved one, not the other; that was his crime. Yet,—so strange a creature is man,—he came back after thirty years, just to see our Lady's grave.'

'What! Are you—'

'I am Mitchell,—Reuben Mitchell.'

MACARIUS THE MONK

BY JOHN BOYLE O'REILLY

In the old days, while yet the church was young,
And men believed that praise of God was sung
In curbing self as well as singing psalms,
There lived a monk, Macarius by name,
A holy man, to whom the faithful came
With hungry hearts to hear the wonderous Word.
In sight of gushing springs and sheltering palms,
He lived upon the desert: from the marsh
He drank the brackish water, and his food
Was dates and roots,—and all his rule was harsh,
For pampered flesh in those days warred with good,

From those who came in scores a few there were
Who feared the devil more than fast and prayer,
And these remained and took the hermit's vow.
A dozen saints there grew to be; and now
Macarius, happy, lived in larger care.
He taught his brethren all the lore he knew,
And as they learned, his pious rigors grew.
His whole intent was on the spirit's goal:
He taught them silence—words disturb the soul;
He warned of joys, and bade them pray for sorrow,
And be prepared to-day for death to-morrow;
To know that human life alone was given
To test the souls of those who merit heaven;
He bade the twelve in all things be as brothers,
And die to self, to live and work for others.
"For so," he said, "we save our love and labors,
And each one gives his own and takes his neighbor's."

Thus long he taught, and while they silent heard,
He prayed for fruitful soil to hold the word.

One day, beside the marsh they labored long,—
For worldly work makes sweeter sacred song,—
And when the cruel sun made hot the sand,
And Afric's gnats the sweltering face and hand
Tormenting stung, a passing traveller stood
And watched the workers by the reeking flood.
Macarius, nigh, with heat and toil was faint;
The traveller saw, and to the suffering saint
A bunch of luscious grapes in pity threw.
Most sweet and fresh and fair they were to view,
A generous cluster, bursting-rich with wine.
Macarius longed to taste. "The fruit is mine,"
He said, and sighed; "but I, who daily teach,
Feel now the bond to practice as I preach."
He gave the cluster to the nearest one,
And with his heavy toil went patient on.

As one athirst will greet a flowing brim,
The tempting fruit made moist the mouth of him
Who took the gift; but in the yearning eye
Rose brighter light: to one whose lip was dry
He gave the grapes, and bent him to his spade.
And he who took, unknown to any other,
The sweet refreshment handed to a brother.
And so, from each to each, till round was made
The circuit wholly—when the grapes at last,
Untouched and tempting, to Macarius passed.

"Now God be thanked!" he cried, and ceased to toil;
"The seed was good, but better was the soil.
My brothers, join with me to bless the day."
But, ere they knelt, he threw the grapes away.